The Grimmest of Grimm

as told by Cyrus Rua

Lysander Press

Published by the Lysander Press, Ontario

First Printing, October 2004
First Mass Market Edition, January 2005
10 9 8 7 6 5 4 3 2 1

ISBN: 0-9737090-0-6

Cover design by Cyrus Rua
Edited by Teri Bishop

Printed in the United States of America.

Table of Contents

Also illustrated by Cyrus Rua:
The Picture of Dorian Gray

For those who trespass against us.

The Grimmest of Grimm

The Boy Who Went Forth to Learn What Fear Was

Illustrated by Cyrus Rua

Gut Kegel und Kartenspiel, 1819

Originally told to the Grimms by Ferdinand Siebert & Dorothea Viehmann nce upon a time, there was a father with two sons. The elder brother was clever and sensible and could handle any situation that faced him, but the younger was dim and could neither learn nor understand much of anything at all.

Whenever people met him, they said to themselves, "What a burden he'll always be to his father!"

If there was anything that needed to be done, the older brother was the one to take care of it, but if their father asked him to fetch something in the evening hours or during the night, and if that meant that he had to pass through the churchyard or some other scary place, he would cry, "Oh, no, father. I can't go there... it gives me the shivers!"

He spoke these words not from laziness, but was indeed afraid.

Sometimes tales scary enough to make

to make one's skin crawl would be told by the fireside at night, and the listeners would say, "It gives me the shivers! It gives me the creeps!" And often times the younger brother would be listening from the corner, but he never understood what they meant. "They're always saying, 'It gives me the shivers! It gives me the creeps!' But it doesn't give me the shivers at all. It must be some sort of trick that I don't comprehend."

One day his father said to him, "Listen boy, you're getting big and strong. It's time you began to earn your keep. Just look how hard your brother works, while you're still a hopeless case."

"I would gladly learn something, father," the boy replied, "If possible, I'd like to learn how to get the shivers, for that is something I know nothing about."

When the older brother heard this, he laughed and thought to himself, 'Oh, Lord, what a dimwit my brother is! He'll never amount to anything. Cut your coat according to your cloth.'

The father sighed and responded, "You're sure to learn all about fear in due time, but it's not going to help you to put food on your plate."

Soon after this time, the sexton came to visit their house, and the father complained about his youngest son, saying that he wasn't capable of doing anything, let alone learning or knowing anything. "Why, when I asked him what he wanted to do for a living, he said he wanted to learn to get the shivers! Have you ever heard of such a thing?"

"If that's all that he wants," the sexton said, "he may learn fear from me. Send him to me, and I'll smooth over his edges." The father was glad to do this, thinking the boy needed to shape up.

So the sexton took the boy to his house, where he was assigned to the ringing of the church bell. A few days passed, and one night the sexton woke the boy at

midnight and told him to climb the steeple and ring the bell.

'Now you'll learn what the shivers are,' the sexton thought, secreting up the stairs ahead of him. When the boy reached the belfry and turned around to reach the rope, he saw a white form standing on the stair across from the sounding hole.

"Who's there?" he cried, but from the figure received no reply. "Answer me!" the boy shouted, "and get out of here, for you've no business here at night."

The sexton remained motionless and silent, for he wanted the boy to think he was a ghost.

The boy shouted again, "If you're an honest man, say something, or I'll throw you down the stairs!"

'He can't really mean that,'

thought the sexton, and remained as stiff and quiet as a stone.

A third time the boy shouted, and still receiving no reply, lunged at the spectre and pushed him down the stairs. The ghost fell ten steps and lay crumpled in the corner. The boy then rang the bell as he had been told, went home to bed, and fell asleep without saying a word.

The sexton's wife waited for her husband for hours, but he never returned. She anxiously woke the boy and asked, "Have you seen my huband? He climbed the steeple before you."

"No," said the boy, "There was someone in the belfry, but he refused to answer me or go away, so I thought he must be some sort of scoundrel and I pushed him down the stairs... I'd feel sorry if it was him."

The sexton's wife ran off to find her husband lying at the foot of the stairs, crying and moaning from his broken legs. She carried him to his bed and rushed off to the boy's father, screaming as she went.

SOME SORT OF SCOUNDREL

"Your boy has caused a horrible accident!" she cried, "He threw my husband down the stairs and broke his legs. Get the worthless lout out of my house!"

Disgusted, the father ran to the sexton's house, where he scolded the boy, "The Devil must have put you up to the Godless tricks you've been playing!"

The boy pled his innocence, "Father, he was just standing there by night as one with evil designs. I didn't know who he was and entreated him three times to answer me or leave."

"You're nothing but trouble!" the father said, "Get out of my sight. I never want to see you again!"

"Gladly, father. But give me until dawn, and I'll go away to learn to get the shivers. That'll teach me a trick or two, and I'll be able to earn a living."

"Learn what lessons you will," replied his father, "Take these fifty talers into the wide world, but tell no one where you came from or who your father is. I'm ashamed of you and shall see you no more."

"As you wish, father. If that's all you desire,

I can easily remember."

At new light's dawning, the boy put the fifty talers into his pocket and stepped out onto the road, muttering to himself, "If only I could get the shivers! If only I could get the creeps!"

A man joined him on the road for some time, and when they had gone a distance together he said to the boy, "Do you see that tree there? That's where seven men were wedded to the ropemaker's daughter and are now learning how to fly. Sit beneath the tree until nightfall and you'll certainly learn how to get the shivers."

"If it is truly as easy as that," the boy said, "you shall have my fifty talers. Come back for me in the morning."

The boy sat beneath the gallows and waited for evening to come. It was cold, and he made a fire, but by midnight the wind blew so sharply

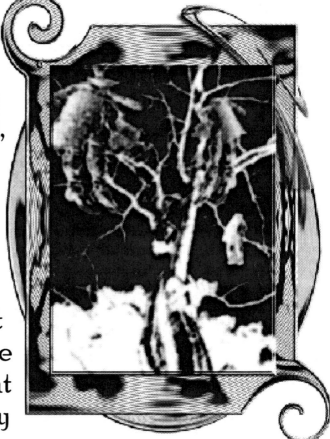

and became so cold that he could not keep warm in spite of the blaze. The wind knocked the hanged men against one another, and they swung back and forth, and the boy thought how cold they must be if he was freezing down by the fire. Feeling sorry for them, he got a ladder and untied them one after another and hauled all seven down to the ground. Then he stirred the fire and set them all around so that they might warm themselves. But they just sat there with- out stirring until their clothes caught on fire.

So he said, "Be careful, or I will hang you up again!"

The dead men, however, did not hear, indeed they were quite silent, and let their rags contin- ue to burn. At this, the boy grew angry and said, "If you will not take care, I cannot help you; I cer- tainly will not let you burn me." And he hung them up again each in turn. Then he sat down by his fire and fell asleep, and the next morning, the man came to him and wanted to have the fifty talers.

"Well, do you know now how to get the shivers?" asked he.

"No," answered the boy, "How could I know? Those lads up there did not open their mouths and were so stupid that they let the few old rags which they did own get burnt."

The man realized that he would not get the fifty talers that day and went away saying, "Such a youth has never come my way before!"

The youth likewise went on his way, and once more began to mutter to himself, "If only I could get the shivers! If only I could get the creeps!"

A carter who was striding behind him heard this and asked, "Who are you?"

"I know not."

"Who is your father?"

"That I may not tell you." the boy said.

"What's that you are always mumbling between your teeth?"

"Oh," replied the youth, "I so wish I could learn to fear, but no one can teach

me how."

"What foolish chatter!" said the carter. "Come along with me, and I will see about a place for you to sleep."

The youth went with the carter, and in the evening they arrived at an inn where they wished to pass the night. Then, at the entrance of the parlour, the youth again said quite loudly, "If only I could get the shivers! If only I could get the creeps!"

The innkeeper heard this and laughed, "If that is your desire, there ought to be a good opportunity for you here."

"Oh, be quiet," said the innkeeper's wife, "so many foolish boys have already lost their lives, it would be a pity and a shame if such beautiful eyes as these should never see the light again."

But the boy said, "However difficult it may be, I will learn it. To get the creeps, indeed have I journeyed forth." He let the host have no rest, until he

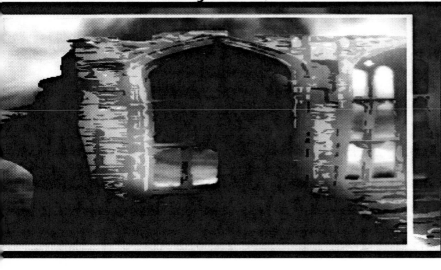

was told that not far away stood a haunted castle where anyone could very easily learn what fear was. He need but remain in it for three nights. The king had promised that he who would venture therein should have his daughter to wife, and she was the most beautiful maiden the sun shone upon. Likewise, in the castle lay great treasures, which were guarded by evil spirits, and these treasures, when freed, would make a poor man rich. Many men had gone into the castle, but as yet none had returned.

The youth went the next morning before the king and said, "By your leave, I will willingly watch three nights in the haunted castle."

The king looked at him, found the boy to his liking, and said, "You may ask for three things to take into the castle with you, but they must be without life."

"Then," replied the youth, "I ask for a fire, a turning lathe, and a carpenter's bench with the knife."

The king had these things carried into the castle for him during the day. Just before nightfall, the youth went up and made himself a bright fire in one of the rooms, placed the carpenter's bench and knife beside it, and seated himself by the turning-lathe.

"If only I could get the shivers!" said he. "But I think I'll not learn it here either."

Toward midnight, he was about to poke his fire, and as he was blowing it, something cried suddenly from one corner: "Meow, meow! How cold we are!"

"You fools!" cried he. "What are you crying about? If you are cold, come and take a seat by the fire and warm yourselves."

No sooner had he spoken when two great black cats came with one tremendous leap and sat down on each side of him, looking ferociously at him with their fiery eyes.

After a short time, when they had warmed themselves, they said, "Comrade, shall we play a game of cards?"

"Why not?" the boy replied. "But first show me your paws."

Thereupon, he seized them by the scruffs, put them on the cutting board, and fastened their feet fast.

"I have looked at your fingers," said he, "and I've lost my desire to play cards." Then he beat them to death and threw them out into the water. But when he had done away with those two and was about to sit down again by his fire, out from every hole and corner came black cats and black dogs with red-hot chains. More and more of them came until he could no longer move, and they screamed terribly and got on his fire, tore it apart, and tried to put it out. He watched them for a while calmly, but when it became so terrible that he could no longer bear it, he seized his cutting-knife, and cried, "Away with you, vermin!" and began to cut them down. Some of them ran away, the others he killed and threw out into the fish-pond. When he 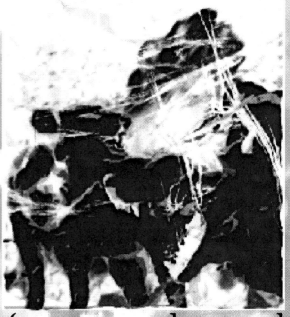 came back, he built up his fire again and warmed himself. As he thus sat, his eyes grew heavy, and he felt a desire to sleep. Then he looked around and saw a great bed in the corner. "That is the very thing I need," said he, and he lay down on it. Just as he was shutting his eyes, however, the bed began to move of its own accord and went over the whole of the castle.

"That's right!" he cried, "but go faster!"

The bed sped on as if six horses were harnessed to it, up and down, over thresholds and stairs, but suddenly, *crash-bang!* it turned over upside down and lay on him like a mountain. He threw the blankets and pillows up in the air, climbed out and said, "Now anyone who would like a ride can have one." And he lay down by his fire, and slept until it was day.

In the morning, the king came, and when he saw the boy lying there on the ground, he thought the evil spirits had killed him and he was dead.

Then he said, "What a pity, for so handsome a man."

Upon hearing this, the youth sat up and declared, "It has not come to that yet."

The king was astonished and very glad, and he asked how the boy had fared.

"Very well indeed," answered he, "one night is past and the other two will pass as well."

Then he went to the innkeeper, who opened his eyes very wide, and said, "I never expected to see you alive again! Have you yet learnt what fear is?"

"No," said he, "it is all in vain. If someone could but tell me!"

The second night, he again went up into the old castle, sat down by the fire, and once more began his old lament, "If only I could get the shivers! If only I could get the creeps!"

When midnight came, an uproar and noise of rumbling about was heard, at first resounding softly but it grew louder and louder. Then it was quiet for a while, until suddenly with a loud scream, half a man came down the chimney and fell before his feet.

"Hullo!" cried he, "You're half missing. This is not enough!"

Then the tumult began again. There was a roaring and howling, and the other half came tumbling down.

"Wait," said the boy, "I will stoke up the fire a little for you." When he had done that and looked around again, the two pieces had joined together to form a hideous man who was now sitting in his place.

"That was no part of our bargain," said the youth, "the bench is mine."

The man tried to push him away, but the youth would not allow that and thrust him off with all his strength and seated himself again in his own place.

Suddenly more men came tumbling down the chimney, one after the other; they brought nine dead men's legs and two skulls and set them up for a frame of bowling. The youth felt a desire to play as well and asked, "Can I play, too?"

"Yes, if you have any money."

"Money enough," replied he, "but your balls are not quite round."

Then he took the skulls and put them in the lathe and turned them till they were round. "Now they will roll much better!" said he. "Huzzah! Now we'll have fun!" He joined their game and lost some of his money, but when the clock struck twelve, everything vanished from his sight. He lay down and fell fast asleep.

The next morning, the king came to inquire about him. "How has it fared with you this time?" asked he.

"I played a game of bowling," he answered, "and have lost a couple of talers."

"Did you not get the shivers?"

"Not at all!" said he, "I have had a wonderful time! If I did but know what it was to shiver!"

The third night he sat down again on his bench and said quite sadly, "If only I could get the shivers! If only I could get the creeps!"

When it grew late, six tall men came in bearing a coffin. He said, "Aha,

that is certainly my little cousin, who died only a few days ago," and he beckoned with his finger and cried out, "Come, little cousin, come."

They placed the coffin on the ground, and he went to it and took the lid off to see that a dead man lay therein. He felt the dead man's face, and it was cold as ice.

"Wait," said he, "I will warm you a bit." He went to the fire, warmed his hand, and laid it on the dead man's face, but he remained cold. Then he took him out and sat down by the fire and laid the corpse on his lap, rubbing his arms that the blood might circulate again. When this, too, was unsuccessful, he thought to himself, "When two people lie in bed together, they warm each other," and carried the cadaver to the bed, covered him up, and lay down beside him.

After a time, the dead man became warm too and began to move. Then said the youth, "See, little cousin, have I not warmed you?"

The dead man, however, got up and shouted "Now I will strangle you!"

What!" responded the boy, "Is that the thanks I get? You shall at once go into your coffin again." He lifted him up, threw him into the coffin, and shut the lid. Then the six men returned and carried him away again.

"I'll never get the shivers!" said the boy. "I shall never learn what fear is as long as I live."

Then a man entered who was taller than all the others and had a terrible look about him. He was old and had a long white beard.

"You wretch," cried he, "I will give you the shivers, for you are about to die!"

"Not so fast," replied the youth. "If I am to die, you would have to catch me."

"I will soon seize you," said the fiend.

"Easy now, do not threaten me. I am as strong as you are, and perhaps even stronger."

"We shall see," said the old man. "If you are the stronger, I will release you. Come, let us try one another."

Then he led the boy by dark passages to a smith's forge, took an axe, and with one blow struck an anvil into the ground.

"I can do better than that," said the youth, and he went to the other anvil. The old man, with his white beard hanging down, drew near to watch. The youth then seized the axe, split the anvil with one blow, and in it caught the old man's beard.

"Now I have you," said the youth. "And it is your turn to die."

He seized an iron bar and beat the old man until he moaned and entreated the youth to stop and promised him great riches. The youth drew out the axe and let him go. The old man led him back into the castle and, in a cellar, showed him three chests full of gold.

"Of these," said he, "one part is for the poor, the other for the king, the third yours."

Just then, the clock struck twelve, and the spirit disappeared, leaving the youth in darkness.

"I shall still be able to find my way out," said he, groping about until he found the way back into his room and slept there by the fire.

The next morning the king came and said, "Now something must have given you the shivers."

"No," he answered, "What could have? My dead cousin was here, and a bearded man came and showed me a great deal of money down below, but no one told me what it was to fear."

Then said the king, "You have saved the castle and shall marry my daughter."

"That is all very well," said he, "but still I do

not know what it is to shiver!"

Then the gold was brought up and the wedding celebrated; but howsoever much the young prince loved his wife and however happy he was, he still sang the same refrain, "If only I could get the shivers! If only I could get the creeps!"

And this at last angered her. Her waiting-maid said, "I will find a cure for him; he shall soon learn what it is to shiver."

She went out to a brook which flowed through the garden and fetched a whole bucketful of minnows.

That night when the young prince was sleeping, his wife pulled the clothes off of him and emptied the bucket full of cold water and minnows over him, so that the little fishes would flap about him. Then he woke up and exclaimed, "Oh, what makes me shiver so? What makes me shiver so, dear wife? Ah! Now I know what it is to shiver!"

The Maiden Without Hands

Illustrated by
Terry Beal

Das Mädchen ohne Hände, 1812,
Originally told to the Grimms by
Marie von Hassenpflug, Dorothea
Viehmann & Johann HB. Bauer

nce upon a time, a miller was slowly falling into poverty, and before long, had nothing to his name but his mill and the large apple tree behind it. One day while on his way to chop wood in the forest, he encountered an old man whom he'd never met before.

"There's no call for you to burden yourself with the cutting of wood," the old man said, "I shall make you a rich man if you promise to give me what is behind your mill."

"That is nothing but my apple tree," thought the miller, and he gave the stranger his promise in writing.

"In three years time, I'll come fetch what's mine." the

stranger said with a cold laugh as he went away.

When the miller returned home, his wife met him at the door and said, "Tell me, dear husband, whence came these riches into our house? All at once I've discovered our chests and boxes are full. No one has brought us these things, and I don't know how it's happened."

"It's all from a stranger I met in the forest," said the miller. "He promised me great riches if I agreed to give him what is behind our mill. We certainly no longer need a large apple tree."

"Oh dear husband!" his wife exclaimed. "This was surely the Devil; he meant not the apple tree but our daughter, who was behind the mill sweeping out the yard."

The miller's daughter was a lovely and pious maiden who passed the next three years in fear of God and without sin. When the time had come and gone, and the day came for the Devil to fetch her, she washed herself clean and drew a circle around her with chalk. The Devil appeared early in the day, but when he could not get near her he angrily said to the miller, "You must take all the water away from her so that she can no longer wash herself. Otherwise, I shall have no power over her."

In his fear of the Devil, the miller did as he was told. The next morning, the Devil returned, but the maiden had wept on her hands and washed them completely clean. Again, the Devil could not get near her and said to the miller in fury, "Chop off her hands! Otherwise I can't touch her."

"How could I chop off the hands of my own dear child?" the miller replied in horror.

"If you don't do it, then you are mine, and I will come for you myself." The Devil replied in a cold voice.

Again in fear of the Devil, the miller promised to obey. To his daughter said he, "My child, if I don't chop off both of your hands, the Devil will take me away. Please help me from my predicament and forgive me the hurt I will cause you."

"Dear father," she replied, "do what you will with me, for I am your child."
She then extended both hands for him to chop off. A third time the Devil came, but she had cried so long on the bloodied stumps that

34

they too were pristine. He was forced to abandon his game, and lost all claim to her.

The miller said to his daughter, "I've gained such wealth because of you and shall see to it that you live in comfort for the rest of your life."

"No, father, I cannot stay here. I'm going away and shall depend on the kindness of strangers to provide me with what-ever I need."

She had her maimed arms bound to her back, and at first light set upon the road and walked the entire day until darkness fell. She rested outside the Royal Gardens, and in the glimmering of the moon, she saw trees full of beautiful fruit, but she could not enter the garden because it was surrounded by a moat. She was very hungry and thought she must eat some of the fruit or else perish. She fell to the earth and prayed to the Lord. Suddenly an angel appeared, and he closed one of the locks in the stream so that the

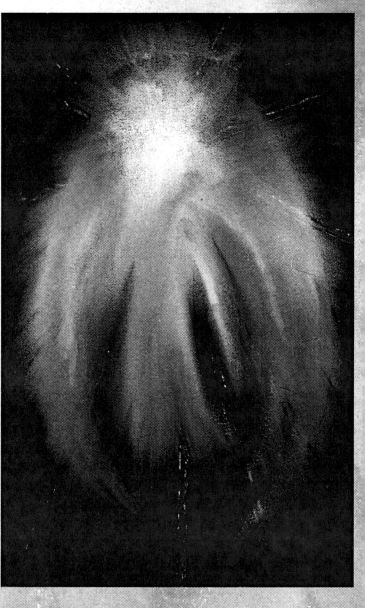

moat became dry and she could walk through it. She entered the garden with the angel by her side.

The girl caught sight of a beautiful tree full of pears, but all of the pears had been counted. Nevertheless, she approached the tree and plucked one of the pears with her mouth to sate her hunger, but only one. The gardener was watching her and thought her a ghost accompanied by an angel, and he was afraid. He kept very still and did not dare to cry out. After she had eaten a pear and her hunger was stilled, she hid in the bushes.

The next morning, the king himself came to the garden and counted his pears. When he found one was missing, he asked the gardener what happened to it, for it was not lying under the tree.

"Last night, a spirit with no hands appeared and plucked one of the pears with its mouth," answered the gardener.

"How did this spirit come over the moat?" asked the king, "and where did it go after it ate the pear?"

"A man in robes as white as snow came down from heaven and closed the lock so that the spirit could walk through the moat. It must have been an angel, and I was afraid to cry out. After the spirit had eaten the pear, it just went away."

The king replied, "I shall keep watch tonight and see if it's as you say." When darkness fell, the king entered the garden, bringing a priest to speak with the spirit. They and the gardener sat beneath the tree and kept watch. At midnight, the maiden came out of the bushes and ate again from the tree, the angel in white by her side. The priest came forth and said to the maiden, "Are you a creature of heaven or of earth? Are you a spirit or a human being?"

"I am not a spirit, but a poor creature forsaken by everyone, save God."

"You may be forsaken by the whole world, child, but you shall not be forsaken by me." said the king.

He took her away to his palace and loved her with all his heart, for she was beautiful and good. He had made for her hands of silver and took her for his wife.

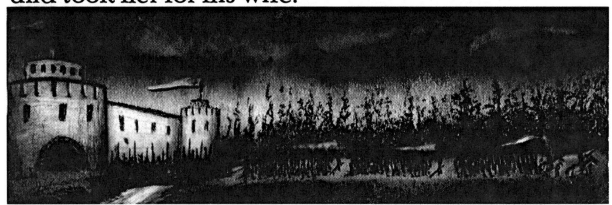

A year came and went, and the king and his men soon went off to war. He placed the young queen in the care of his mother, telling her to contact him when their child was born and to love and protect her.

Very soon after, a fine looking son was born. The king's mother immediately wrote to him the joyful news, but on the way to deliver it, the messenger fell asleep by a brook, exhausted from the journey. The Devil then appeared. Still grudging the pious young queen, he exchanged the queen mother's letter with one that said the queen had birthed a changeling. When the king read the letter, he was horrified and distressed, but wrote to his mother that she should care for and protect his bride until his return.

The messenger began his return journey with the letter, stopping to rest again at the very same spot and fell asleep. Once again, the Devil appeared and put a new letter with the king's seal upon it into the pocket of the messenger that said the queen and her child should be killed. The dowager was aghast when she received the letter and could not believe it. She wrote to the king again, but received the same response because the Devil replaced the letters with forgeries each time. The last letter commanded the queen mother to save the tongue and eyes of the queen as proof his will had been done.

The old woman wept at the thought of shedding such innocent blood. During the night, she had a doe slaughtered and the tongue and eyes pickled to save. She then said to the queen, "I cannot allow you to be killed as the king commands, but you can no longer remain here. Go out into the wide world with your child and never return."

She tied the child to the queen's back and the young woman departed with tears in her eyes.

Entering the great forest, she fell to her knees and prayed to God. The Lord's angel came before her and led her to a small cottage with a sign hanging in front that said "Free Lodging for Everyone." A maiden in snow white robes came out from the cottage and said, "Welcome, Your Majesty," and took her inside. She untied the young prince and offered him her breast that he may drink. She

then laid him upon a beautifully made bed.

"How did you know that I am the queen?" asked the piteous girl.

"I am an angel sent forth by the Lord to care for you and your child," replied the maiden in white.

The queen remained seven years in the cottage and was well cared for. By her own piety and the grace of God, her hands that had been chopped off grew back again.

Finally, the king returned from the wars to see his wife and heir. His old mother began to weep and said, "You wicked man, why did you order me to kill two innocent souls?" She angrily slapped the Devil's forged letters upon the table and displayed for him the pickled tongue and eyes. "Your will's been done."

At the sight of them, the king burst into bitter tears at the thought of his poor little wife and the son he would never see. His old mother was roused and took pity on him.

"Take comfort," said she, "They yet live. These are but the tongue and eyes of a doe. I took the child and tied him to your queen's back and sent them out into the wide world, never to return."

"I shall search as far as the sky is blue without

food or drink until I find my dear wife and child," declared the king, "unless they have been killed or died from hunger in the meantime."

Seven years the king wandered, searching every crag and valley. Unable to find them, he feared his family had perished. During this time he neither ate nor drank, but God kept him alive. Finally, he came to the great forest and discovered the little cottage with the sign "Free Lodging for Everyone." Then the maiden in white came out, took his hand, and led him inside.

"Welcome, Your Majesty," said she and asked him whence he came.

"I've been wandering these seven long years in search of my wife and son, but I cannot find them."

The angel offered him food and drink, but he refused, asking only rest and shelter. He laid down to sleep and covered his face with a handkerchief. Then the angel went into the room where the queen was sitting with her son, whom she had named Sorrowful. "Take your child into the next room," said the angel. "Your husband has come".

The queen went into the room where the king lay, and the handkerchief fell from his face.

"Sorrowful," said she, "Pick up your father's handkerchief and put it back on his face."

The child picked up the handkerchief and placed it over the king's face. In his sleep, the king heard all of this, and he pleasured in making it drop to the floor again.

"Mother," the impatient child said, "how can I cover my father's face when I have no father on this earth? I've learned to pray to 'Our Father Who Art in Heaven,' and you've told me that my father was our good Lord. This wild man is not my father."

The king heard this and, rising, asked the young queen who she was.

"I am your wife," she replied, "and this is our son, Sorrowful."

"You cannot be her," said the king, "for my wife had silver hands."

"Our merciful Lord has restored natural hands to me." answered the queen.

The angel returned to the sitting room to retrieve the silver hands and presented them to the king. He was now certain that these were indeed his dear wife and child, and he kissed them and was happy.

"A heavy burden has been lifted from my mind." said he.

After the Lord's angel joined them in one last meal, they went home to join the king's old mother. Everywhere there was rejoicing as the king and queen renewed their wedding vows and lived happily ever after.

The Robber Bridegroom

Illustrated
by Katy Rose

Der Rauberbrautigam, 1812.
Originally told to the Grimms by Marie Hassenpflug

here once was a miller who had a beautiful daughter, and when she was grown up, he wanted to see her well married and provided for. He thought to himself, "I will give her to the first suitable man who comes and asks for her hand."

Not long after, a suitor appeared who seemed to be very rich, and since the miller could find no fault with him, he promised him his daughter. But the girl did love the man as a girl ought to care for her betrothed. Nor did she feel that she could trust him, and she could not look at him nor think of him without her heart shuddering with dread.

One day said he to her, "You've never visited me, though we have been engaged for some time."

"I do not know where your house is," the maiden replied.

"My house is out in the dark forest," said he.

She tried to make excuses by saying that she would not be able to find the way thither, but her bridegroom only replied, "You must visit next Sunday, for I have already invited guests, and I will strew ashes along the path that you may not mistake the way."

When Sunday came, and the time neared for the

maiden to depart, a feeling of dread came over her which she could not explain. She filled her pockets with peas and lentils to sprinkle on the ground and mark the path as she went along. On reaching the entrance to the forest she found ashes had been spread, and she followed them while throwing down some peas on either side of her at every step she took. She walked nearly the whole day until she came to the deepest, darkest part of the forest. There she saw a solitary house, looking so dark and dreary that it did not please her at all. She stepped inside, but not a soul was to be seen, and a great silence reigned therein. Then suddenly a voice cried out:

"Turn back, turn back,
young maiden fair,
Linger not in this murderers' lair."

The maiden looked up and saw that the voice came from a bird in a cage hanging on the wall. Again it cried out:

"Turn back, turn back, young maiden fair,
Linger not in this murderers' lair."

The bride passed on from room to room of the house, finding all empty, and she saw no one. At last she went down to the cellar, and there sat a very, very old woman, who could not keep her head from shaking. "Can you tell me if my betrothed husband lives here?" asked the girl.

"Oh, you poor child," answered the old woman, "You've no idea where you are. This is a murderers' den! You think yourself a promised bride, and that your marriage will soon take place, but the only marriage you'll celebrate will be with death. Just look! Do you see that large cauldron of water which I am obliged to set to boil? When they have you in their power they will chop you to pieces without mercy, and cook you and eat you, for they are cannibals! If I do not take pity on you and save you, you will be lost forever."

The old woman then led her behind a large barrel, where nobody could see her. "Be as still as a mouse," said she, "Neither move nor speak, or it will be all over with you. Tonight, when the robbers are all asleep, we will escape. I have long been waiting for an opportunity."

The words were hardly out of her mouth when the godless crew returned, dragging another maiden with them. They were all drunk, and paid no attention to her cries and lamentations. They gave her wine to drink, three full glasses, one white wine, one red, and one yellow, and with that, her heart burst in two. Then they tore off her fine clothing, laid her on a table, cut her beautiful body into pieces, and sprinkled the pieces with salt.

Behind the barrel, the poor bride trembled, for she saw what a terrible fate had been intended for her by the robbers. One of them now noticed a gold ring still remaining on the little finger of the mur~dered maiden, and as he could not draw it off easily, he took a hatchet and cut the finger off. But the fin~ger sprang into the air, and fell behind the cask into the lap of the bride. The robber took a candle and began looking for it, but he could not find it.

"Have you looked behind the large barrel?" asked one of the others.

Now the old woman called out, "Come and eat your suppers, and let the thing be until tomorrow; the finger's not going to run away from you."

"The old woman's right," said the robbers, and they stopped look~ing for the finger and sat down to eat. The old woman then mixed a sleeping draught into their wine, and before long they were all lying on the floor of the cellar, fast asleep and snoring. As soon as the bride heard this, she came from behind the cask, and had to step over the bodies lying in rows upon the floor.

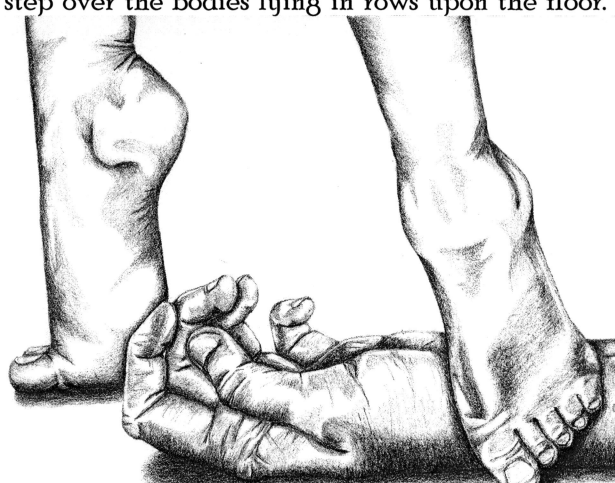

And every moment she was filled with renewed dread lest she should awaken them, but she got safely through with the help of God. She and the old woman went upstairs, opened the door, and scampered as fast as they could from the murderers' den. They found the ashes scattered by the wind, but the peas and lentils had sprouted, and unfurled, guiding the way in the moonlight. They walked the whole night through, and it was morning before they reached the mill. Then the maiden told her father all that had happened.

When the day of the wedding celebration came, the bridegroom appeared, as did a large company of friends and relations the miller had taken care to invite. As they sat at the feast, each guest was asked to tell a story; the bride, though, remained still and did not utter a word.

"Well, my dear," said the bridegroom, turning to her, "is there no tale you know? Tell us something."

"I will tell you a dream, then," said the bride. "I went alone through a forest and came at last to a house. Not a soul could I find within, except for a bird in a cage on the wall cried out:
'Turn back, turn back, young maiden fair,
Linger not in this murderers' lair.'
"...and again a second time it said these words."
"My darling, it was only a dream."

"I went through all the rooms of the house, finding all empty, and everything was so grim and mysterious. At last I went down to the cellar, where I found a very, very old woman, who was bobbing her head. I asked her if my betrothed lived here, and she answered, "Ah, you poor child, you have come to a murderers' den; your bridegroom does indeed live here, but he will chop you up without mercy and afterwards cook and eat you."

My darling, it was only a dream.

"The old woman hid me behind a large barrel, and no sooner was I hidden than the robbers returned home, dragging a young maiden behind them. They gave her all sorts of wine to drink, white, red, and yellow, and with that she died."

"*My darling, this was only a dream!*"

"Then they tore off her resplendent clothes, and cut her beautiful body into pieces and sprinkled salt upon it."

"*My darling, this is only a dream!*"

"One of the robbers saw that there was a gold ring still left on her finger, and he had difficulty pulling it off, so he took a hatchet and cut her finger off. The finger sprang into the air and fell behind the barrel into my lap...And here is the finger with the ring!"

With these words the bride produced the finger and showed it to the assembled guests.

The bridegroom, who had grown deadly pale during the narration, jumped up and attempted to flee, but the guests seized him and held him fast. They delivered him to the magistrate, and he and all of his murderous band were executed for their shameful crimes.

The Blacksmith and the Devil

Illustrated by Karen Petroff

Der Schmied und der Teufel, 1822,
Traditional tale of Hessia

nce upon a time there was a blacksmith who really enjoyed his life, squandering his money and carrying on many lawsuits. In a short matter of years, he hadn't a heller left to his name.

"Why should I suffer myself the world any longer?" he asked himself and went into the forest to hang himself from a tree. Just as he was sticking his head through the noose, a man with a long white beard came out from behind a tree, a large book in hand. "Blacksmith, blacksmith," said he, "Lay your name upon my tome and for ten long years your life will be blessed. But at ten years and a day you will be mine and I shall come fetch you."

"Who are you?" asked the blacksmith.

"I am the Devil."

"Forsooth? And what can you do?"

"My power is great," the self-named Devil replied, "I can make myself as tall as a fir tree or as small as a mouse."

"Why, this I must see!" said the smith, "for to see is to believe."

Thereupon the bearded man grew and grew and soon was as tall and mighty as a fir tree. Then with a great clap of his hands he shrank to the size of a field mouse.

Impressed, the blacksmith said, "Give me your book, Devil, and it shall have my name."

When the ink of the blacksmith's signature had dried upon the page, the Devil said, "Now home with you, where you'll find chests and boxes filled to the brim. I will come for you in ten years and a day, and will visit you once in that time besides."

Home the blacksmith went, and he found that all of his pockets, drawers and chests were filled with ducats, and no matter how much he took from them they never became empty and his fortune was never reduced in the least. He began again his merry life in earnest, invited all his friends to join him, and was the merriest fellow in the land.

After a few years had passed, the Devil came and visited as he had promised. Upon his departure, he gave the blacksmith a magic leather sack. Whoever jumped into the sack would not be able to get out again until the blacksmith himself released them. The blacksmith had a great deal of fun with it, indeed.

When the ten years had passed, the Devil returned to him and said, "Time's up, and you are now mine. Prepare yourself for your journey."

"Certainly," said the blacksmith, swinging his leather sack over his shoulder and walking away with the Devil.

Soon they came to the spot in the forest where they had met, where the blacksmith had meant to hang himself and where their fateful bargain had been struck. "I want to be certain that you are truly the Devil," the blacksmith said, "make yourself as large as a fir tree and as small as a mouse again if you can."

"I can." Said the Devil, and grew and grew and soon was as tall and mighty as a fir tree. Then with a great clap of his hands he again shrank to the size of a field mouse, whereupon the blacksmith grabbed him and tossed him into the magic leather sack. Then the blacksmith broke off a stick from a nearby tree, tossed the sack to the ground and began mercilessly beating the Devil, who screamed piteously and ran back and forth within the sack, finding no escape.

Finally, the blacksmith said, "I will release you if you give me the page from your large book upon which I wrote my name."

The Devil refused, but another round of fierce beatings with the stick soon convinced him. The sheet was ripped from the book, and the Devil returned to hell cursing him~ self for being beaten and deceived.

Back to his smithy the blacksmith went, and continued to live happily as long as it was God's will. But the years took their toll, and he became old and weak as all men must, and when he heard death upon his doorstep, he ordered two long nails and a hammer to be placed within his coffin.

This was done as he willed, and upon his death he approached the gates of heaven and knocked. But Saint Peter refused to open the gates to him because he had lived in league with the Devil. When the blacksmith heard this, he turned around and went straight to hell. The Devil would not let him enter either, for he had no desire for this man in hell where he would only make a spectacle of himself.

The blacksmith was angry and caused a great din at hell's gate, and curious, a little daemon peeked out of the gate to see what the commotion was about. Quickly, the blacksmith grabbed him by the nose and nailed him solidly to the gate of hell with one of the nails he had with him. The sound of the little daemon screaming like a wildcat drew another daemon to the gate. He too stuck his head out, and the alert blacksmith grabbed him by the ear and nailed him to the gate right next to the first little daemon.

Now they both let out such terrible cries that the old Devil himself came running, and when he saw the two little daemons  nailed solidly to the gate he became so terribly angry that he wept and jumped about.

The Devil ran up to the dear Lord in heaven and told Him that He must admit the blacksmith to heaven for there was nothing that he, the Devil, could do. If the blacksmith nailed all the daemons by their ears and noses, then the Devil would no longer be master in hell. If the dear Lord and Saint Peter wanted to be rid of the Devil, then they would have to let the blacksmith enter heaven.

So now the blacksmith sits there quietly and peacefully, but I don't know how the two little daemons were able to free themselves.

Cinderella

Illustrated by Terry Beal

Aschenputtel, 1812
Originally told to the Grimms by an anonymous woman in Marburg.

he wife of a rich man fell sick; and when she felt that her end drew nigh, she called her only daughter to her bed-side, and said, 'Always be a good girl, and I will look down from heaven and watch over you.' She then shut her eyes and departed, and was buried in the garden; the little girl went every day to her grave and wept, and was always good and kind to all about her.

Winter came and covered the grave with a little white blanket, and by the time that the sun had shaken it off again in the spring the rich man had taken a second wife who brought with her two daughters of her own; they were fair in face but foul in heart, and it was now a sorry time for the poor little girl.

"What does the stupid goose want in the parlour?" said they; "they who would eat bread should first earn it; away with the kitchen-maid!" Then they took away her fine clothes, and gave her an old grey frock to put on, and wooden shoes. "Just look at the proud princess in her finery!" they laughed as they led her into the kitchen.

There she was forced to do hard work; to rise early before daylight, to bring the water, to make the fire, to cook and to wash. Besides that, the sisters did all they could to torment her, pouring lentils into the

the hearth ashes and forcing her to pick them out. In the evening when she was exhausted from working, they took away her bed, and she was made to lie by the hearth among the ashes; and as this, of course, made her always dusty and dirty, they called her Cinderella.

It happened once that the father was going to the fair, and asked his stepdaughters what he could bring them.

"Fine clothes," said the first.

"Pearls and diamonds." cried the second.

"And you, child," said he to his own daughter, "what will you have?"

"The first twig, dear fa-ther, that brushes against your hat when you turn your face homewards is all I desire." Said she.

So he bought for the first two the beautiful 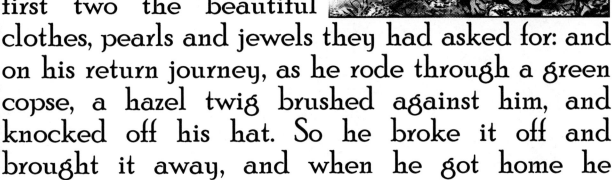 clothes, pearls and jewels they had asked for: and on his return journey, as he rode through a green copse, a hazel twig brushed against him, and knocked off his hat. So he broke it off and brought it away, and when he got home he gave it to his daughter. She thanked him and took it to her mother's grave and planted the twig upon it, weeping so much that it was watered with her tears. There it quickly grew and became a fine tree. Three times every day she would sit beneath it and weep and pray, and soon a little bird came and built its nest upon the tree, and talked with her, and watched over her, and brought her whatever she wished for.

Now it happened that the king of that land held a feast, which was to last three days; and all the beautiful young girls were invited; out of those who came to it his son was to choose for himself a bride. When the stepsisters learned that they too had been summoned, they called to Cinderella.

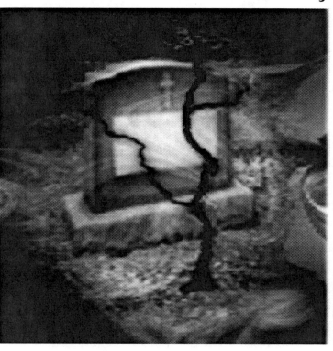

"Now, comb our hair, brush our shoes, and tie our sashes for us, for we are going to dance at the king's feast." Cinderella obeyed, but wept, for she thought to herself, she should so have liked to have gone with them to the ball; and at last she begged her stepmother's permission to go.

"You, Cinderella!" said she, "You're all dusty and dirty, you have nothing to wear, no clothes at all, and you cannot even dance; you want to go to the ball?"

To Cinderella's continuing pleas, said she at last, "I will throw this dishful of lentils into the ash-heap, and if in two hours time you have picked them all out, you shall have my permission to go."

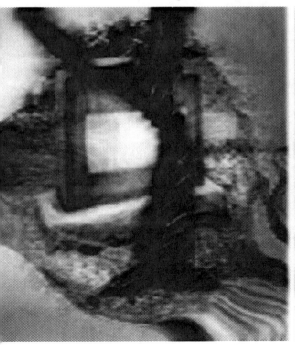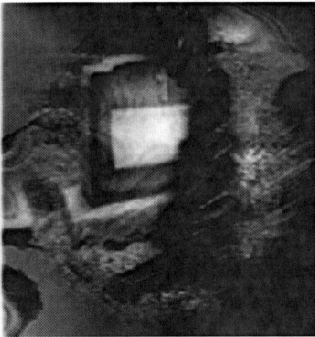

Then she threw the lentils down among the ashes, and the little maiden ran out the back door into the garden, and cried out:

"Turtledoves and pigeons fly
and all the birds beneath the sky,
fly to me quick and help me pick
the best ones for the little pot
and all the rest may be your lot."

Two white doves came flying in at the kitchen window, next came two turtle-doves, and after them came all the little birds under heaven, chirping and fluttering in, and they settled down into the ashes. And the little doves bobbed their heads down and began to *peck, peck, peck,* and then the others began to *peck, peck, peck* and put all the good lentils in a bowl, but left the ashes. Long before the end of an hour the work was quite done, and all flew out again at the windows. Overjoyed at the thought that she should now attend the ball, Cinderella presented the bowl to her stepmother. But the step-mother said, "No, no, you slut, you have no

clothes, and cannot dance; you shall not go."

To Cinderella's growing tears, said she, "If you can in one hour's time pick two of those dishes of peas out of the ashes, you may go too." And thus she thought she should at least get rid of her. So she shook two dishes of peas into the ashes.

But the maiden went out into the garden at the back of the house, and cried out as before:

"Turtledoves and pigeons fly
and all the birds beneath the sky,
fly to me quick and help me pick
the best ones for the little pot
and all the rest may be your lot."

Two white doves came flying in at the kitchen window, next came two turtle-doves, and after them came all the little birds under heaven, chirping and fluttering in, and they settled down into the ashes. And the little doves bobbed their heads down and began to *peck, peck, peck;* and then the others began to *peck, peck, peck* and put all the good peas into the bowls, but left the ashes. Before half an hour's time all was done, and out they flew again. Happy because she thought that she must now be allowed to attend the ball, Cinderella carried the bowls to her stepmother. But her mother said, "It is all of no use, you cannot go for you have no clothes, cannot dance, and you would only put us to shame." She turned her back on Cinderella and off she went with her two daughters to the ball.

When all had departed, Cinderella went sorrowfully and sat down under the hazel-tree, and cried out:

"Shake and tremble, hazel-tree,
Gold and silver over me!"

Then her friend the bird flew out of the tree, and

brought a gold and silver dress for her, and silken slippers embroidered with silver. She hastily put them on, and followed her sisters to the feast. But they did not know her, and thought it must be some strange princess, she looked so fine and beautiful in her  rich clothes; and they never once thought of Cinderella, thinking that she was of course at home in the dirt picking lentils from the ashes.

Now, the prince soon approached Cinderella, took her by the hand and danced with her, and no one else. Indeed, he never left her side and when anyone else came to ask her to dance, said he, "This lady is dancing with me."

Thus they danced late into the night, and when she wanted to go home, the prince said, "I shall escort you." For he wanted to see whose daughter the beautiful maiden was. But she slipped away from him, unawares, and ran into her father's dovecote. Now the prince waited until her father came home, and told him that the unknown maiden, who had been at the feast, had hid herself in the dovecote. But when they had broken down the door they found no one within, and as they came back into the house, Cinderella was lying, in the ashes in her dirty frock, and her dim little oil lamp was burning on the mantle of the chimney. For she had run as quickly as she could

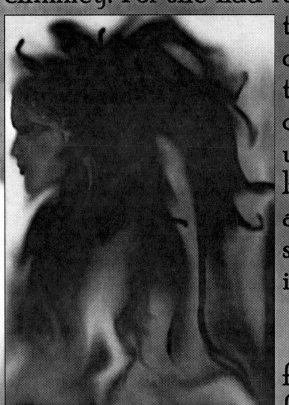

through the dovecote and on to the hazel-tree, had taken off her beautiful clothes, and laid them upon the grave, that the bird might carry them away, and had seated her-self again amid the ashes in her little grey frock.

The next day when the feast began again, and her father, mother, and sisters were gone, Cinderella went to the hazel-tree, and cried out:
"Shake and tremble, hazel-tree,
Gold and silver over me!"

And the bird came and brought a more

splendid dress than the one before. And when she appeared at the ball in it, everyone wondered at her beauty. The prince had been waiting for her. And took her by the hand, and danced with her and no one else, and when anyone asked her to dance, said he as before, "This lady is dancing with me."

When night came and she wanted to go home, the prince followed her as before, that he might see into what house she went: but she sprang away from him all at once into the gar- den be- hind her fa- ther's house. In this garden stood a fine large pear-tree full of ripe fruit; and Cinderella, not knowing where to hide herself, jumped up into it as nimbly as a squirrel. Then the king's son lost sight of her, and could not determine where she had gone, but waited until her father came home, and said to him, "The un- known lady who danced with me has slipped away, and I think she must have sprung into the pear-tree."

The father thought to himself, "Can that be Cinderella?" And he had an axe brought and they chopped down the tree, but found no one upon it. And when they came back into the kitchen, there lay Cinderella among the ashes; for she had slipped down on the other side of the pear tree, and carried her beautiful clothes back to the bird at the grave, and then put on her little grey frock.

On the third day, when her father and mother and sisters were gone, Cinderella went again into the garden, and cried out to the tree:

"Shake and tremble, hazel-tree,
Gold and silver over me!"

Then her kind friend the bird brought a dress more magnificent and stunning than all the others, with slippers of gold. When she came to the feast, no one knew what to say for wonder at her beauty. The prince again danced with nobody but her, and whenever anyone asked her to dance, said he, "This lady is my partner, sir."

When night came she wanted to go home; and the king's son would go with her, and said to himself, 'I will not lose her this time;' but, however, she

again slipped away from him, though in such a hurry he could not follow her. This time, however, the prince had prepared for her tricks and had coated the stairs with pitch. When Cinderella ran down the stairs, her left slipper was stuck and she had to abandon it. The prince picked it up and saw that it was small and dainty and made of gold.

The next morning, the prince took the shoe to Cinderella's father, declaring that no one should be his wife but the maiden whose foot fit the golden shoe. Both the stepsisters were overjoyed to hear it, for they had beautiful feet, and had no doubt that they could wear the golden slipper. The eldest went first into the room where the slipper was, and wanted to try it on, and her mother stood by her side. However, her big toe could not fit into it, and the shoe was altogether too small for her. So her mother gave her some pruning shears, and said, "Cut the toe off, dearest. When you are queen you'll not have to walk." So the maiden lobbed off her big toe, and thus forced on the shoe, and went before the prince. Then he took her for his bride, and set her beside him on his horse, and rode away with her toward the castle.

But on their way home they had to pass by the hazel-tree that Cinderella had planted; and on the branch sat a little dove singing:

"Looky, look at the tiny shoe
Made for another, but stolen by you.
Blood flows out from the false bride,
Oh, Prince, an imposter there rides by your side."

Then the prince got down and looked at her foot and he saw, by the blood that streamed from it, what a trick she had played him. So he turned his horse round, and brought the false bride back to her home, and said, "This is not the right maiden; let the other sister try and put on the slipper."

Then the other sister went into the room and got her toes into the shoe, but her heel was too large. So her mother handed her a butcher's knife and said to her, "Trim the edges, my dear. Once you're queen you'll not need to walk." The maiden sliced off a chunk of her heel, forced her foot into the slipper, and swallowing her pain, presented herself before the prince. And he set her as his bride by his side on his horse and rode away with her.

But when they came to the hazel tree, the little dove sat there still, and sang:

"Looky, look at the tiny shoe,
Made for another, but stolen by you.
Blood flows out from the false bride,
Oh, Prince, an imposter there rides by your side."

Then he looked down, and saw that the blood streamed so profusely from the shoe that her white stockings were stained red. So he turned his horse and brought her also back again.
"This is not the true bride," said he to the father; "have you no other daughters?"
"No," said the father, "there is only a little dirty Cinderella here, the child of my first wife; she cannot possibly be the bride."
The prince told him to send the girl to him, but the stepmother said, "She is much too dirty; she will not dare to show herself."

However, the prince demanded to see her, and Cinderella was called. She first washed her face and hands, and then went in and curtsied to him, and he handed her the golden slipper. Then she took her heavy wooden shoe off her left foot, and put on the golden slipper and it fit her as if it had been made for her. And when he drew near and looked at her face he knew her, and said, "This is my true bride!"

But the mother and both the sisters were horrified, and turned pale with anger as he took Cinderella on his horse and rode away with her. And when they came to the hazel tree, the white dove sang:

"Looky, look at the tiny shoe,
Stolen by others but made for you.
No blood needs flow from your right bride,
Oh, Prince, your princess rides by your side."

And when the dove had done its song, it came flying and perched upon her right shoulder, and there it remained.

Upon their wedding day, the two stepsisters came to the palace to share in Cinderella's good fortune. When the bridal couple set out for the church, the oldest stepsister was to the right and the youngest to the left. Suddenly, the dove swooped down from the heavens and pecked out the left eye of each of them. And after the joyous ceremony, the oldest stepsister was on the right and the youngest on the left. Then the dove came again and pecked out the other eye of each sister.

Thus were they blinded forever due to their wickedness.

The Death of the Hen.

Illustrated by Luc Hébert

Von dem Tode des Hühnchens 1812

Originally told to the Grimms by Clemens Brentano and Wilhelm Engelhardt nce upon a time a hen and cock went to the nut hill, and they agreed that whichever one of them found a kernel would share it with the other. Soon the hen found a very big nut, but she said nothing because she wanted to eat the kernel all by herself. The nut was so large, however, that she could not swallow it, and

it got caught in her throat. Fearing that she would choke to death, she screamed, "Rooster! Run as fast as you can and fetch me some water, or I will choke to death!"

The cock ran as fast as he could to the well and said, "Well, you must give me some water, for the hen is lying on the nut hill choking to death!"

"First you must run to the bride," the well replied, "and get some red silk for me."

So the rooster ran to the bride, crying, "Oh, bride, I need from you your red silk to trade with the well who will give me some water to take to the hen who is lying on the nut hill where she is about to choke to death."

The bride answered, "My silk you may have, but you must first fetch me my wreath that got caught in the branches of the willow."

Now, the cock ran to the willow and took the wreath from the branch and returned it to the bride. In return, the bride gave him some red silk, and the rooster brought it to the well, who gave him water in exchange. The rooster took the water to the hen, but by the time he reached her she had already choked to death and lay before him cold and motionless.

The rooster became so forlorn that he loosed a

loud cry, and all the animals came and mourned her. Six mice built a little wagon that was to carry the hen to her grave, and when it was finished, they harnessed themselves to it, allowing the rooster to be their driver.

Along the way, they met the fox, who asked, "Where are you going, Rooster?"

"I'm off to bury the hen."

"May I ride with you?"

"Yes, but you are heavy so you must sit in the back," said the rooster, "If you sat in front, my horses would fall and the wagon would crack."

So the fox took a seat in the back where he was soon joined by the wolf, the stag, the lion, and all of the animals of the forest, and thus they continued their journey until they came to a brook.

"However shall we cross?" cried the rooster.

A straw was lying near the brook that said, "I'll lay myself across and you can drive over me." But as soon as the mice touched the straw bridge, the straw slipped and fell into the water and the six mice went tumbling after and drowned. A hot piece of coal witnessed the tragedy and said, "I'm big enough to lay myself across and let you ride over me."

Then the hot coal also laid itself across the water, but it unfortunately grazed its surface. It soon began hissing, and quickly extinguished and died. When a stone saw that, it took pity on the cock and his party and offered its help. It lay down across the water and the rooster himself pulled the wagon across.

He reached the other side with the dead hen and wanted to help the others from the back of the wagon, but there were too many of them, and the wagon slipped back into the water where they all fell in and drowned.

Now the rooster was all alone with the dead hen, and he dug a grave for her. He laid her down and made a cairn on top of the grave where he then sat down and grieved until he too died.

And then everyone was dead.

The Singing Bone

Illustrated by Jon Ferrll

Der Singende Knochen, 1812
Originally told to the Grimms by Dortchen Wild

nce upon a time, there was a land in great dismay because a wild boar was flattening the farmer's fields, slaughtering cattle, and tearing people to shreds with its tusks. The king promised a huge reward to anyone who could rid the kingdom of this blight. But the beast was so strong and mighty that no one dared enter the forest where it dwelled. Finally, the king proclaimed that whosoever killed the wild boar would receive his only daughter for a wife.

There were two brothers, sons of a poor man, who were living in that kingdom, and they declared themselves willing to face the challenge.

The eldest brother, a cunning and clever man, acted from pride, and the younger, innocent and naïve, acted from the goodness of his heart.

"Enter the forest from opposite sides," advised the king, "and you'll be more certain of finding the great beast."

The elder entered the forest from the west and

the younger from the east. After the younger had walked for a time, a little dwarf bearing a black spear approached him and said, "I give you this spear for I can see that you have a good and pure heart. With this you may attack the wild boar, and it will be unable to reach you."

The boy thanked the dwarf, hung the spear over his shoulder, and continued walking without fear. Soon he saw the beast, and when it charged, he stuck out his spear, and in its rage the boar ran into it with such force that its heart was sliced in two. The boy flipped the monster over his shoulder and went to deliver it to the king.

When he exited the forest, he saw a house where people were dancing, drinking, and having a grand time. His older brother had gone there thinking that the boar would not escape him and wished to fortify his courage with rum. When he saw his younger brother coming out of the forest and carrying his prize, his envious and wicked heart gave him no peace.

"Come inside, dear brother," he cried, "rest and refresh yourself with a glass of wine."

Excitedly, the youth went inside and told his

brother about the good dwarf who had given him
a spear to kill the boar. The older brother kept him
there until late in the evening and they together
departed. In the darkness they came to a bridge
spanning a brook, and when the younger brother
was halfway across, the elder gave him such a hard
blow from behind that he fell down dead. The
brother buried him under the bridge, took the boar,

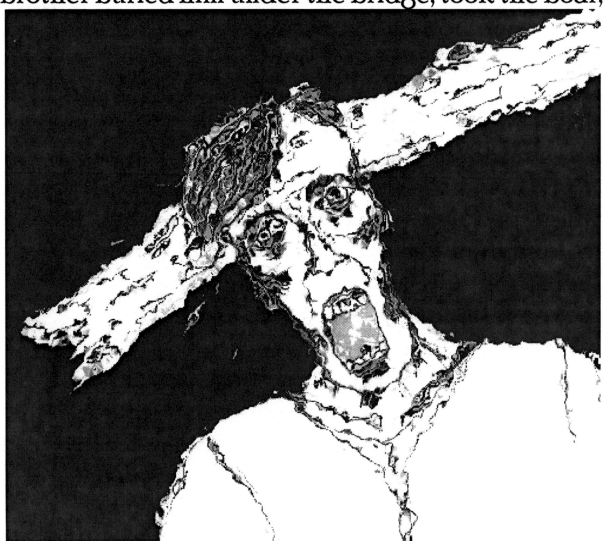

and presented it to the king, who gave him his daughter for his wife. When the younger brother never returned, the older said, "The boar must have ripped him apart." And everyone believed him.

After many years had passed, the shepherd was driving his flock across the bridge and saw a little Bone, snow white, lying beneath it. He snatched up the Bone and carved it into a mouthpiece for his horn. When he blew into it the first time, the shepherd was startled as the little Bone began to sing of its own volition:

> "Oh shepherd, how could you know
> You are blowing on my Bone!
> My brother killed me years ago,
> And left me to rot under the bridge alone.
> The boar he took and left me for dead
> The king's fine daughter for to wed."

"What a remarkable horn," said the shepherd, "to sing by itself! I shall take it to the king."

Before the king, the little horn again sang its song. Understanding full well, the king had the ground under the bridge exhumed. When the skeleton of the murdered man was revealed, the wicked brother could not deny his deed, and he was sewn up in a sack and drowned. And the bones of his murdered brother were laid to rest in a beautiful grave in the churchyard.

The Mouse, the Bird & the Bratwurst

Illustrated by
Cyrus Rua

Von dem Mäuschen, Vogelchen, und der Bratwurst, 1812.

Originally told to the Grimms by Hans Michael Moscherosch.

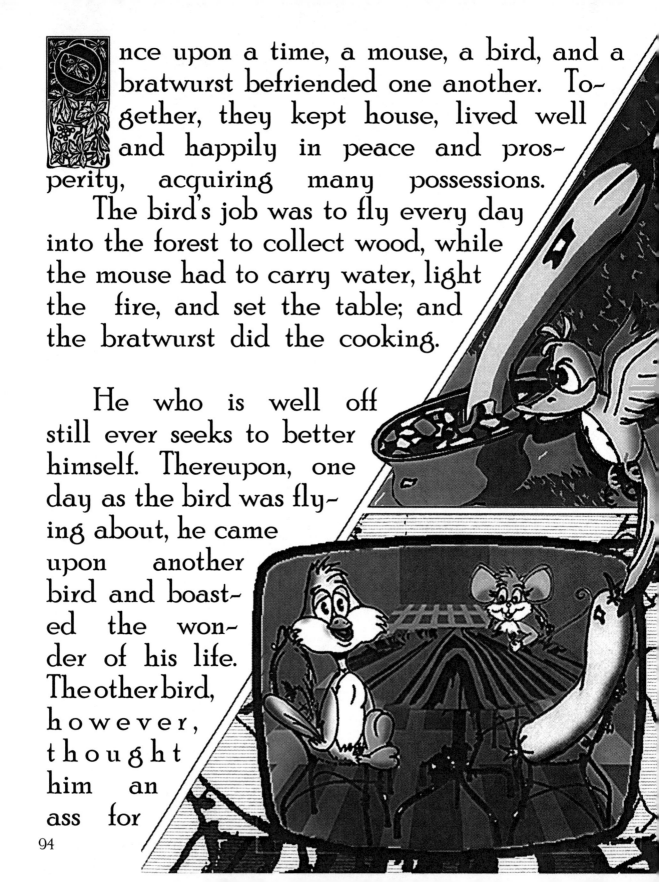

nce upon a time, a mouse, a bird, and a bratwurst befriended one another. Together, they kept house, lived well and happily in peace and prosperity, acquiring many possessions. The bird's job was to fly every day into the forest to collect wood, while the mouse had to carry water, light the fire, and set the table; and the bratwurst did the cooking.

He who is well off still ever seeks to better himself. Thereupon, one day as the bird was flying about, he came upon another bird and boasted the wonder of his life. The other bird, however, thought him an ass for

94

working so hard while the others enjoyed themselves at home. For after the mouse had made her fire and carried her water, she could lounge in the parlour until it was time for her to set the table. The bratwurst merely stood about watching the pot, and when dinnertime neared, she slid through the stew or vegetables, and thus was everything greased and salted and ready to eat. When the bird returned home and laid down his heavy load, they sat to supper, and when they had eaten their fill, slept soundly until the next morning. Such was their splendid life. The next day, the bird, because of his new friend's advice would go no more into the wood. He told his companions that he had played servant long enough and had been made the fool. He insisted that they at once try other arrangements. While the mouse and bratwurst argued in earnest, the bird would not be denied. They drew straws forthwith, and the lot fell upon the bratwurst to carry the wood from then on, the mouse became cook, and the bird was to fetch water.

What happened?

The bratwurst trudged off toward the woods,

the little bird lit the fire, and the mouse put on the pot and waited for the bratwurst to return with the next day's wood. But the bratwurst stayed so long in the wood that they both feared something untoward had occurred. The bird flew out to find 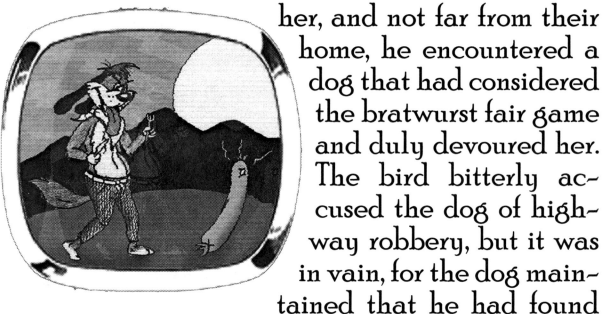 her, and not far from their home, he encountered a dog that had considered the bratwurst fair game and duly devoured her. The bird bitterly accused the dog of highway robbery, but it was in vain, for the dog maintained that he had found forged letters on the bratwurst on which account its life was to him forfeited.

Filled with sorrow, the bird carried the wood home himself, with a troubled tale to tell. The mouse was distressed at the telling, but they both agreed to do their best to remain together. The bird therefore set the table while the mouse prepared the food. The little mouse wished to season the meal as the bratwurst had always done, by jumping into the pot and rolling and creeping amongst the vegetables, but before she was even halfway through them she became mired, losing her hair, skin, and life in the attempt.

When the bird came to carry up the meal, there was no cook. In his distress, he scattered the wood about everywhere, calling and searching for the mouse, but no cook was to be found. Owing to his distraction and carelessness, the wood soon caught fire and the house went up in flames. The bird hastened to fetch some water, but the bucket slipped from his grasp and plummeted into the well, dragging the little bird with it.

Unable to recover himself, he was left to drown.

The Three Army Surgeons

Illustrated by Kelly Levy

Die Drei Feldscherer, 1815,
Originally told to the Grimms by Dorothea Viehmann

hree army surgeons who thought they knew their profession perfectly were travelling about the world, and they came to an inn where they wanted to spend the night. The innkeeper asked whence they came, and whither they were going.

"We are roaming about the world and practising our profession."

"Well, show me what you can do," said the innkeeper. The first surgeon said that he would cut off his own hand and reattach it the next morning. The second said he would tear out his heart and replace it the next morning. The third said he would gouge out his eyes and put them back in their sockets the next morning.

"If you can do that," said the innkeeper, "you have indeed learnt everything of your profession."

Truth be told, however, they had a salve, which immediately healed any wound upon which it was rubbed, and they carried it with them wherever they went. So they cut the hand, heart, and eyes from their bodies as they had vowed, laid them on a plate, and gave them to the innkeeper. The innkeeper gave it to a servant girl who was to set it in the cupboard for safekeeping.

Unknown to all, however, the girl had a lover who was a soldier, and when the innkeeper, the three army surgeons, and everyone else in the house were asleep, the soldier came and wanted something to eat. The girl opened the cupboard and brought him some food, and in her rapture, forgot to shut the cupboard door again. She sat down at the table by her lover, and began chatting away. While she sat so contentedly there with no thought of misfortune, the cat came creeping in, found the cupboard open, and carried off the hand and heart and eyes of the three army surgeons. When the soldier had done eating, and the girl was about to clear the table and shut the cupboard, she saw that the plate which the innkeeper had given her to take care of was empty. Filled with dread, said she to her lover, "Ah, miserable girl, what shall I do? The hand is gone; the heart and the eyes are gone too! What will become of me in the morning?"

"Be easy," said he, "I will help you out of your trouble. There is a thief hanging outside on the gallows. I will go and cut off his hand. Which hand was it?"

"The right one."

Then the girl gave him a sharp knife, and he went and cut the poor sinner's right hand off and brought it to her. After this, he caught the cat and gouged its eyes out, and now naught but the heart was missing.

"Have you not been slaughtering, and are not the dead pigs in the cellar?" asked he.

"Yes," said the girl.

"Well, that's perfect," said the soldier, and he went down and fetched a pig's heart.

The girl placed all together on the plate and put it back in the cupboard. After her lover departed, she went quietly to bed.

In the morning when the three army surgeons got up, they told the girl to fetch the plate upon which the hand, heart, and eyes were lying. She brought it to them, and the first fixed the thief's hand on and smeared it with his salve, and it promptly grew to his arm. The second took the cat's eyes and put them in his empty sockets. The third fixed the pig's heart firm in the place where his own had been, and the innkeeper stood by, admired their skill, and said he had never yet seen such a thing before. Indeed, he would sing their praises and recommend them to everyone. Then they paid their bill and con~ tinued on their journey.

As they were on their way, the surgeon with the pig's heart did not stay with the other two at all, but rooted about in corners with his nose as pigs do. The others wanted to hold him back by his coat~tails, but that did no good. He tore himself loose and ran wher~ ever the dirt was deepest.

The second surgeon also behaved very strangely. He rubbed his eyes, and said to the others, "Comrades, what has happened? These are not my eyes. I can't see at all. Will one of you lead me, so that I do not fall?"

Then with difficulty they travelled on until

evening, when they reached another inn. They went into the bar to-gether, and there at a table in the corner sat a rich man counting out his money. The surgeon with the thief's hand walked about him, made a few jerky movements with his arm, and at last when the stranger turned away, snatched at the pile of money and took a handful from it. One of his companions saw this and said, "Comrade, what are you doing? You must not steal. Shame on you!"

"Alas!" said he, "I cannot stop myself. My hand twitches, and I am forced to snatch things whether I will or not."

After this, they lay down to sleep, and their room was so dark it was impossible to see one's hand in front of one's face. Suddenly, the surgeon with the cat's eyes awoke, aroused the others, and said, "Brothers, look! Do you see the little white mice running about?"

The other two sat up, but could see nothing. Then said he, "Things are not right with us; we have turn to the innkeeper, for he has deceived us."

not received again what was ours. We must return to the innkeeper, for he has deceived us."

So the three army surgeons went back the next morning and told the host they had not received their proper organs. One had gotten a thief's hand, the second cat's eyes, and the third a pig's heart. The innkeeper said that the serving girl must be to blame and was going to call her, but when she had seen the three coming, she had run out by the back door and never returned. The three said he must give them a great deal of money, or they would set the house on fire.

The innkeeper gave them what he had and whatever he could raise, and the three went away with it. It was enough for the rest of their lives, but they would rather have had their own rightful organs.

The Goose Girl

Illustrated by
Cyrus Rua
and Terry Beal

Die Gänsemagd, 1815

Originally told to the Grimms by Dorothea Viehmann

he king of a great land died, and left his queen to care for their only child. This child was a daughter, who was very beautiful; and her mother loved her dearly and was very kind to her. When she grew up, she was betrothed to a prince who lived in a distant kingdom, and as the time drew near for her to be married, she got ready to set off on her journey to his country. Then, the queen her mother packed up a great many precious items, jewels, gold, and silver; trinkets, fine dresses, and, in short, everything that became a royal bride and her dowry. She also gave her a chambermaid to ride with her and give her safely into the bridegroom's hands. And each received a horse for the journey, and the princess's horse was called Falada, and could speak.

When the time came for them to set out, the queen went into her bedchamber, took a little knife, and cut her finger to make it bleed. She then placed a white handkerchief underneath her finger and let three drops of blood fall upon it and gave it to the princess.

"Take care of it, dear child," said she, "for it is a charm that may be of use to you on the road." Then she took a sorrowful leave of the princess, and she

put the handkerchief into her bosom, got upon her horse, and set off on the journey to her bridegroom's kingdom.

One day, as they were riding along by a brook, the princess began to feel very thirsty: and said she to her maid, "Get down, and fetch me some water in my golden cup out of yonder brook, for I want to drink."

"Nay," said the chambermaid, "if you are thirsty, get off yourself, and stoop down by the water and drink. I shall not be your servant any longer."

And the princess was so thirsty that she got down and knelt over the little brook and drank. But she was frightened, and dared not ask for her golden cup. She wept and said, "Alas! What will become of me?"

And the three drops of blood responded:

"Alas! Alas! If thy mother knew it,
Sadly, sadly, would she rue it."

But the princess was very gentle and meek, so said she nothing and got upon her horse again. They rode farther on their journey, until the day grew so warm and the sun so scorching, that the princess began to feel very thirsty again, and at

last, when they came to
a river, she forgot her
maid's nasty words, and
said, "Pray get down, and
fetch me some water to
drink in my golden cup."

But the maid an-
swered her, even spoke more haughtily than
before, "Drink if you will, but do so alone. I shall
not be your servant."

The princess was so thirsty that she got off her
horse and lay down and held her head over the
running stream, crying, "What will become of me?"

And the handkerchief answered her again:

"Alas! Alas! If thy mother knew it,
Sadly, sadly, would she rue it."

And as she leaned down to drink, the handkerchief fell from her bosom, and floated away down-
stream. In her fear she did not see it, but her maid
saw it and was very glad, for she knew the charm,
and she saw that the poor bride could be in her
power. So when the princess had done drinking
and would have got upon Falada again, the

maid said, "I shall ride upon Falada, and you may have my nag instead." So she was forced to give up her horse, and soon afterward, to take off her royal clothes and put on her maid's shabby ones.

At last, as they drew near the end of their journey, the treacherous servant threatened to kill her mistress if she ever told anyone what had happened. But Falada saw it all and took good note of it.

Then the waiting-maid got upon Falada, and

the true bride rode upon the wretched nag, and they went on in this way until at last they came to the royal court. There was great joy at their coming, and the prince ran to meet them. He lifted the maid from her horse, thinking she was the one who was to be his wife; she was led upstairs to the royal chamber, but the true princess was told to stay in the court below.

Meanwhile, the old king peered out the window, and when he saw her in the courtyard, he thought her very pretty, and too delicate for a waiting-maid, so he went up into the royal chamber to ask the bride who it was she had brought with her, that was thus left standing in the court below.

"I picked her up along the way for the sake of company on the road," said she; "Pray, give the girl some work to do that she may not be idle."

The old king had no work for her but at last said he, "I have a lad who takes care of my geese; she may go and help him."

Now the name of this lad was Conrad, and the true princess had to help him tend the geese.

Soon after, the false bride said to the prince, "Dear husband, pray do me one piece of kindness."

"Of course I will," said the prince.

"Summon the knacker to cut off the head of the

horse I rode upon, for it was very unruly and plagued me sadly on the road." But the truth was, she was very much afraid that Falada should some day speak and tell all she had done to the princess. She carried her point, and the faithful Falada was killed, but when the true princess heard of it, she wept and offered the knacker a gold coin to nail up Falada's head against the large dark gate of the city through which she had to pass every morning and evening, that there she might still see him sometimes. The slaughterer said he would do as she wished, and he cut off the head and nailed it up under the dark gateway.

Early the next morning, as she and Conrad drove the geese through the gate, said she sorrow-fully: "Falada, Falada, I see you hanging there."

And the head answered:

"Princess, princess is that you?
Alas! Alas! If thy mother knew it,
Sadly, sadly, would she rue it."

Then they went out of the city and drove the geese on into the fields. And when she reached the meadow, she sat down upon a bank there and let down her waving locks of hair, which were all of pure gold. When Conrad saw it glitter in the sun, he ran up and would have pulled some of the strands out, but she cried:

"Blow, ye winds, blow,
Make Conrad's hat go!
Flow, breezes, blow!
Make him after it go,
Over valleys and rocks,
Away should it whirl,
Until my fair golden locks
Are all combed and curled!"

Then there came a gusting wind, so strong that it blew off Conrad's hat into the fields, and he had to run after it. By the time he came back, she had done combing and curling her hair and had put it up again safely, and he couldn't get a single strand of it. Then he was very angry and sulky and would not speak to her at all. Thus they tended the geese until it grew late in the evening, and then drove them homeward.

The next morning, as they were going through the dark gate, the poor girl looked up at Falada's head, and cried:

"Falada, Falada, I see you hanging there."
And the head answered:

"Princess, princess is that you?
Alas! Alas! If thy mother knew it,
Sadly, sadly, would she rue it."

Then they drove on the geese, and she sat down again in the meadow and began to comb out her hair as before. Conrad ran up to her and wanted to take hold of it, but she cried out quickly:

"Blow, ye winds, blow,
Make Conrad's hat go!
Flow, breezes, blow!
Make him after it go,
Over valleys and rocks,
Away should it whirl,
Until my fair golden locks
Are all combed and curled!"

Then the winds came and whisked away his hat;

and off it flew a great way, over the hills and far away, so that he had to run after it. And when he came back, she had long since bound up her hair again, and all was safe and he could not get a single strand. Thus they tended the geese until evening.

In the evening after they came home, Conrad went to the old king and said, "I do not wish that strange girl to help me keep the geese any longer."

"Why?" asked the king.

"Because, instead of doing any good, she does naught but torment me all day long."

Then the king ordered him tell him what she did, and Conrad said, "When we go in the morning through the dark gate with our flock of geese, she cries and talks with the severed head of a horse that hangs upon the wall, and says:

"Falada, Falada, I see you hanging there."

And the head answers:

"Princess, princess is that you?
Alas! Alas! If thy mother knew it,
Sadly, sadly, would she rue it."

Thus Conrad went on telling the king what had happened upon the meadow, how his hat was blown away and how he was forced to run after it, leaving his flock of geese to themselves. But the old king told the boy to drive the geese out again the next day, and when morning came, he placed himself behind the dark gate and heard how the girl spoke to Falada, and how Falada answered. Then he went into the field and hid himself in a shrub by the meadow's side. And he soon saw with his own eyes how the goose girl and the goose boy drove the flock of geese and how, after a while, she let down her hair that glittered in the sun. And then he heard her say:

> "Blow, ye winds, blow,
> Make Conrad's hat go!
> Flow, breezes, blow!
> Make him after it go,
> Over valleys and rocks,
> Away should it whirl,
> Until my fair golden locks
> Are all combed and curled!"

And quickly came a gale of wind, and carried away Conrad's hat, and away went Conrad after it, while the girl calmly went on combing and curling her hair. All this was observed by the old king, and he went home without being seen. When the little goose girl came back in the evening, he called her aside and asked her why she did all those things, but she burst into tears and said, "That I must not tell you or any man, or I shall lose my life. Such is the oath I swore under open skies."

His insistences were futile, and though he gave her no peace, she would not talk.

Then said he, "If you'll not speak to me, allow the iron stove there be wit- ness to your sorrows."

After the king departed, she crawled into the iron stove and began to weep and lament. "Here am I," said she, "forsaken by the world and yet a king's daughter still. My place is stolen by a chamber- maid, while I must labour as a goose girl! Alas, if my mother knew it, sadly, sadly would she rue it!"

The old king stood beside the stovepipe outside and listened to what she said. When her bitter tears abated, he reentered the room and ordered her out of the stove. The king ordered royal clothes be put upon her and gazed on her with wonder, for she was so beautiful. Then he called his son and told him that he had but a false bride who was merely a chambermaid, while the true bride stood by. And the young prince rejoiced when he saw her beauty and heard how meek and patient she had been, saying nothing to the usurper.

The king ordered a great feast for all his court. The bridegroom sat at the head of the table, with the false princess on one side and the true one on the other. But nobody knew her again, for her beauty was quite dazzling to their eyes, and she did not seem at all like the little goose girl for all her finery.

When they had eaten and drank, and were very merry, the old king said he would tell them a tale. So he began and told all the story of the prin-cess, as if it was one that he had once heard; and he asked the chambermaid what she thought ought to be done to anyone who would behave thusly.

"She would deserve nothing better," said this false bride, "than that she should be stripped naked and thrown into a barrel stuck round with sharp nails, and that two white horses should drag her through the streets until she was dead."

"Thou art the very w o m a n !" cried the old king, "and as thou hath judged thyself, so shall it be done to thee."

When the sentence was carried out, the young prince was then wedded to his true bride, and they reigned over the kingdom in peace and h a p p i n e s s for all of their lives.

The Poor Boy in the Grave

Illustrated by Jon Ferril

Der Arme Junge im Grab, 1843

Originally told to the Grimms by Ludwig Aurbacher

nce upon a time, there was a poor shepherd boy whose parents had died. He had been placed in the home of a rich man who had been charged with his care. But the man and his wife were cold and wicked in their hearts and lived a miserly and envious existence in spite of their great wealth. They would spare not even the tiniest morsels of food; hence, the boy received more beatings than food on his plate.

One morning, he was responsible for the care of the hen and her chicks, but the hen snuck through the hedge accompanied by her young, where-upon a hawk swooped upon her and carried her away through the air.

The boy loosed a mighty scream, "Thief! Scoun-drel!" But his cries did little for his benefit, influ-encing the hawk not at all to release his prey and gaining the attention of the man who fell into such a black rage upon finding the loss of his hen that he gave the boy such a thrashing that he was left bedridden for days. Whereupon, he was charged with the care of the chicks without the hen, a difficult task, for they ran all about without order or reason. The smartest course, the lad determined, was to bind them all together with twine so that the hawk would be unable to spirit any away from him. Alas, he was very much mistaken. When he soon fell into sleep, exhausted from his exertions and lack of food, the hawk came and snatched away one of the chicks. The others, tied to the first, followed into the sky. The hawk then landed on a treetop and devoured them all.

Upon his return and witness of the misfortune, the man beat the boy so mercilessly that it was many days before he was again able to leave his bed.

When finally the boy returned to his feet, the man said,

"You're too unbearably stupid for a chicken keeper. Perhaps you'll fare better as my messenger." And he sent the boy to the magistrate, bearing a basket of grapes and a letter. En route, the boy became so overcome with thirst and hunger that he ate two of the grapes.

Upon receipt, the judge read the letter, counted the grapes, and proclaimed that two of them were missing. The boy confessed that he had been quite compelled by hunger and thirst and was responsible. The judge wrote a letter to the boy's stepfather, ordering again the same number of grapes, and yet again the boy was charged with their delivery and another letter for the judge. When the lad was again overcome with hunger and thirst, he could not but help himself to two more grapes. Before doing so, however, he took the letter from the basket and hid it under a stone that it may not bear witness and again betray him. Nonetheless, the judge took him to account for the missing grapes.

"But how could you discover this?" asked the boy, "I hid the letter beneath a stone so that it could not know."

The judge laughed piteously at such simple-mindedness and sent a letter in return, warning the man to give the boy better treatment and more food and drink. He also advised the man to teach the boy the difference between right and wrong.

"I shall indeed show you the difference," said the cold man. "If you would eat, then you must also work, and you'll sufficiently learn the error of your ways through beatings."

The day that followed had the man giving the boy an extremely difficult task. He was to cut several bundles of hay for the horses, and the man told him harshly, "If I find that the hay is not chopped in five hours time upon my return, I shall beat you until you cannot move a bone in your body."

The man went to the fair in the company of his wife and maid, leaving but a small piece of bread for the boy, who set to work with all of his might. In the heat, he removed his little coat and discarded it into the hay. In his haste and zeal, he mistakenly chopped it into pieces. He became aware of his mishap much too late to repair any damages. "Ah!" said he, "It's over for me now. That wicked man threatens not idly, and when he sees what I have done, he shall beat me to death. But I would rather take my own life."

The lad had overheard the man's wife once claim to have a jar of poison beneath her bed, but truly told, she said this but to discourage others, for the jar was filled with honey. The boy crawled beneath the bed, removed the jar, and ate every drop.

"People say," the lad mused, "that death tastes bitter, but I find it sweet. No wonder the lady always wished herself dead."

Whereupon, he sat himself down and prepared to die, but instead of weakening, he found himself strengthened by the nourishment. "It must not have been strong enough." He thought, "but my step-father has said that there is in the closet a bottle of poison for the flies. This will bring about my death."

Neither was this poison, but Hungarian wine, and the boy took the bottle and drank it dry. "This death also tasted sweet," said he, and when soon after the wine mounted his brain and made him dizzy and his stomach turn, he believed his end was near. "I feel I am going to die," said he. "I shall go upon the churchyard and find myself a grave."

He staggered forth, and lay himself in a freshly dug grave, feeling his senses fail him more by the moment. From a nearby tavern came the sounds of a marriage celebration, and when the lad heard the music, he believed himself in paradise and lost all consciousness.

The poor lad never again awoke, for the potent wine and shock of cold indeed took his life, and he there remained in the grave he had chosen for himself.

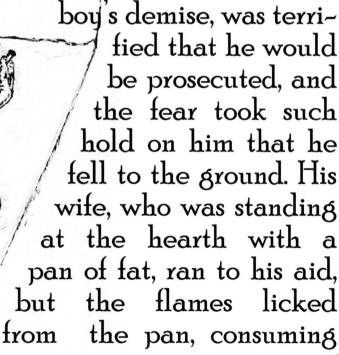

The wicked man, upon receiving news of the boy's demise, was terrified that he would be prosecuted, and the fear took such hold on him that he fell to the ground. His wife, who was standing at the hearth with a pan of fat, ran to his aid, but the flames licked from the pan, consuming

 the entire house, and it was some few hours before it had been reduced to ash.

For the entirety of their lives, the man and his wife were tormented by guilt and spent their days in poverty and misery.

The Brothers 12

Illustrated by Kathryn McLaughlin

Der Zwölf Brüder, 1812

Originally told to the Grimms by Julia and Charlotte Ramus

nce upon a time, there was a king and a queen who lived happily together and had twelve children, all boys. One day, the king said to his wife, "If the thirteenth child that you are about to bear us is a girl, the twelve boys shall die, so she may have all the wealth and that the kingdom may be hers alone."

He even had twelve coffins made, which were already filled with shavings. In each lay a little death pillow, and he had them taken into a locked-up room. He gave the key to the queen and bade her not to speak of it to anyone.

The mother, however, now sat and lamented all day long, until the youngest son, Benjamin, who was named from the bible and who was always with her, said, "Dear mother, why are you so sad?"

"Dearest child," said she, "that I may not tell you."

But he let her have no peace until she went and unlocked the room, and showed him the twelve coffins already filled with wood shavings.

Then she said, "My dearest Benjamin, your father has had these coffins made for you and for your eleven brothers, for if I bring a little girl into the world, all of you are to be killed and buried in them." She wept while she was saying this, and the son comforted her and said, "Weep not, dear mother, we will save ourselves and escape this place."

"Then," said she, "go into the forest with your eleven brothers, and let one of you keep constant watch from the tallest tree, looking ever toward the castle tower. If I give birth to a little boy, I will put up a white flag, and then you may safely return. But if I bear a daughter, I will hoist a red flag, and then you must flee as quickly as you are able. And may the good Lord protect you. Every night will I pray for you to be able to warm yourselves by a fire in the winter and that you do not suffer the heat by summer."

After she had given her sons her blessing, they went forth into the forest. They each kept watch in turn and sat on the highest oak and looked toward the tower. When eleven days had passed and the turn came to Benjamin, he saw that a flag was being raised. It was, however, not the white, but the blood-red flag which announced that they were all to die. When the brothers heard that, they were very angry and said, "Are we all to suffer death for the sake of a girl? We swear that we will avenge ourselves and wheresoever we find a girl, her red blood shall flow."

Thereupon, they went deeper into the forest where it was the darkest, and there they found a little bewitched hut, which was standing empty. "Here we will dwell," said they, "and you Benjamin, who are the youngest and weakest, shall stay at home and keep house. We others will go out and search for food."

Then they went into the forest and shot hares, wild deer, birds, and pigeons, and whatsoever was fit to eat. This they took to Benjamin, who had to prepare it for them in order that they might still their hunger. They lived together ten years in the little hut, and the time passed quickly for them.

The baby their mother the queen had given birth to was now grown into a little girl. She was good of heart and fair of face and had a golden star upon her forehead. One day, when there was a great deal of washing to be done, she saw twelve men's shirts among the things and asked her mother, "To whom do these twelve shirts belong, for they are far too small for father?"

Her mother answered with heaviness in her heart, "Dear child, these belong to your twelve brothers."

Said the maiden, "Where are my twelve brothers? I have never heard of them before."

"God alone knows where they are," replied she. "They are wandering about the world." Then she took the maiden and opened the secret chamber for her, and showed her the twelve coffins with the shavings and the death pillows. "These coffins," said she, "were destined for your brothers, who went away secretly before you were born." And she related to her how everything had happened.

Then said the maiden, "Dear mother, weep not, I will go and seek my brothers."

So she took the twelve shirts and went straight into the great forest. She walked the whole day, and in the evening, she came to the bewitched cottage. When she entered it, she found a young boy, who asked, "Whence do you come, and whither are you bound?" And he was astonished that she was so beautiful, wore royal garments, and had a star on her fore- head.

"I am a king's daughter," she an- swered, "and am seek- ing my twelve brothers. I shall walk as far as the sky is blue until I find them." She showed him the twelve shirts, and Benjamin realized that she was his sister.

"I am Benjamin," said he, "your brother."

And she began to weep for joy, and Ben- jamin wept also, and they kissed and embraced each other with the greatest love. But after this said he, "Dear sister, there is still a problem. We brothers have agreed that every maiden whom we meet shall die because we have been obliged to leave our kingdom on account of a girl."

"Then," said she, "I will willingly die, if by so doing I can save my twelve brothers."

"No," answered he, "you shall not die. Seat yourself beneath this tub until our eleven brothers return, and then I will soon come to an agreement with them."

She did as she was told, and when it was night, the others came back from the hunt and found their meal ready. After they sat down at the table and began eating, they asked, "What news is there?"

Said Benjamin, "Don't you know?"

"No," they answered.

He continued, "You have been in the forest all day and I have stayed at home, yet I know more than you do."

"Tell us!" they cried.

"I shall if you but promise me that the first maiden who meets us shall not be killed."

"Yes!" they all cried. "She shall have mercy, only do tell us!"

Then said he, "Our sister is here." And he lifted up the tub, and the king's daughter came forth in her royal garments. She had a golden star on her forehead, and she was beautiful, delicate and fair.

Then they all rejoiced and kissed and loved her with all their hearts.

Now she stayed at home with Benjamin and helped him with the work. The eleven went into the forest and caught game, deer, birds and pigeons, and whatever was fit to eat, and the little sister and Benjamin took care to make it ready for them. She sought for the wood for cooking and herbs for vegetables and put the pans on the fire so that the dinner was always ready when the eleven came. They likewise kept order in the little house and put beautiful white clean coverings on the little beds, and the brothers were always contented and lived in great harmony with her.

Once upon a time, the two at home had prepared a wonderful feast, and when they were all together, they sat down and ate and drank and were full of joy. There was a little garden next to the bewitched house wherein stood twelve lily flowers, of a sort called student-lilies. She wished to give her brothers happiness, so she plucked the twelve flowers and thought she would present each brother with one while at dinner. But at the very moment that she plucked the flowers, the twelve brothers were

changed into ravens and flew away over the forest. The house and garden vanished likewise.

And now the poor maiden was alone in the wild forest, and when she looked around, an old woman was standing near her who said, "My child, what have you done? Why did you not leave the twelve white flowers growing? They were your brothers, who are now forevermore changed into ravens."

The maiden said, weeping, "Is there no way of saving them?"

"Naught but one," said the woman, "and that is so hard that you will not save them by it. You must be mute for seven years and may not speak or laugh. If you speak one single word and only an hour of the seven years is wanting, all is in vain, and your brothers will be killed by that one word."

"Then," said the maiden with all her heart, "I know with certainty that I shall set my brothers free." And she went and sought a high tree and seated herself in it and began spinning, and neither spoke nor laughed. Now, it so happened that a king was hunting in the forest. He had a great greyhound which ran to the tree on which the maiden was sitting and sprang about it, whining and barking at her.

Then the king came by and saw the beautiful

princess with the golden star on her brow, and he was so charmed with her beauty that he called to ask her if she would be his wife. She made no answer, but nodded a little with her head. Then he climbed up the tree himself, carried her down, placed her on his horse, and took her home. The wedding was celebrated with great splendour and joy, but the bride neither spoke nor smiled.

When they had lived happily together for a few years, the king's mother, who was a wicked woman, began to slander the young queen, and said to the king, "This woman you've brought back with you is nothing but a common beggar! Who knows what wicked mischief she's been secretly plotting? Even if she be dumb and not able to speak, she still might laugh for once. Those who do not laugh must have bad consciences."

At first the king would not believe it, but the old woman accused her of so many evil things for so long, that, at last, the king let himself be persuaded and sentenced her to death. A great fire was lighted in the courtyard in which she was to be burned, and the king stood above at the window and looked on with tearful eyes, for he still loved her, be she evil or no.

When she was bound fast to the stake and the fire was licking at her clothes with its red tongue, the last instant of the seven years expired. Suddenly, a whirring sound was heard in the air, and twelve ravens came flying toward the courtyard and swooped downward. The instant they touched the earth, they became again her twelve brothers, whom she had saved.

They tore the fire asunder, extinguished the flames, set their dear sister free, and kissed and embraced her. And now as she dared to open her mouth and speak, she told the king why she had been mute and had never laughed.

The king rejoiced when he heard that she was innocent, and they all lived in great unity until their death. The wicked queen mother was taken before the judge and put into a barrel that was filled with boiling oil and venomous snakes.

She indeed died an evil death.

The Fitchers Fowl

Illustrated by Benchaoço

Fitcher's Vogel 1812

Originally Told to the Grimms by Friederike Mannel and Dortchen Wild nce upon a time, there was a wizard who used to assume the form of a poor man and went begging to houses to capture pretty girls. No one knew whither he carried them, for none ever returned.

One day, he appeared before the door of a man who had three beautiful daughters. He looked like a poor, weak beggar and carried a basket on his back as though to collect charitable gifts in it. He begged for some food, and when the eldest daughter came out to hand him a piece of bread, he needed but touch her to magically compel her to jump into his basket. Thereupon, he rushed away with great strides and carried her away to his house in the centre of a dark forest. Everything in the house was magnificent, and he gave her whatsoever she could possibly desire.

"My darling," he said to her, "thou wilt certainly be happy with me, for thou hast everything thy heart may desire."

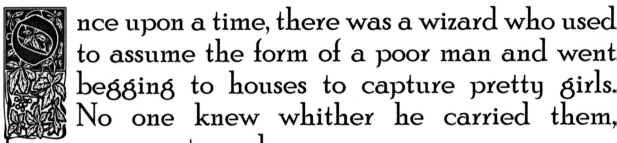

Days passed and soon he said, "I must journey forth and leave thee alone for a short time. Here are the keys of the house; thou mayst go eve~ rywhere and look at everything except i n t o

144

one room, which this little key here opens. There I forbid thee to go on pain of death." He likewise gave her an egg and said, "Preserve the egg carefully for me and carry it about with thee, for a great misfortune would arise from its loss."

She took the keys and the egg and promised to obey him in everything. When he was gone, she explored the house from top to bottom. The rooms shone with silver and gold, and she thought she had never seen such great splendour. Finally, she came to the forbidden door. She wished to continue past it, but curiosity overcame her. She examined the key, which looked like any other, put it in the keyhole and turned it a little, and the door sprang open. But what did she see when she entered? A great bloody basin stood in the centre of the room, and therein lay human corpses hewn to pieces. Next to it was a block of wood with a gleaming axe lying upon it.

She was so horrified that she dropped the egg that she held into the basin. She got it out and washed the blood off, but in vain, for the blood

145

reappeared in an instant. She washed and scraped,
but she could not get rid of the stain.

It was not long before the wizard came back from
his journey, and the first things he demanded were
the keys and the egg. She returned them to him,
trembling as she did so, and he saw at once
by the red spots on the egg that she had been
in the bloody chamber.

"Since thou hast gone into the room against my
will," said he, "thou shalt go back into it against thine

own. Thy life is ended."

He threw her down, dragged her along by the hair, cut her head off on the block, and chopped her into pieces so that her blood flowed about the floor. Then he threw her into the basin with the others.

"Now I shall fetch myself the second daughter," said the wizard.

Once again, he went to the house in the guise of a poor man and begged. When the second daughter brought him a piece of bread, he caught her like the first, by merely touching her. He carried her away, but she did not fare better than her sister, succumbing too to her curiosity, opening the door of the bloody chamber, and atoning with her life upon the wizard's return.

Then he went and fetched the third sister, but she was clever and cunning. After he had given her the keys and the egg and departed, she put the egg away with great care, and then she examined the house. At last she, too, came upon the forbidden chamber. Alas, what did she behold! Her two dear sisters lay there in the basin, cruelly murdered and chopped in pieces.

She began to gather their limbs together and arrange them in order: head, body, arms, and legs.

When nothing further was wanting, the limbs began to move and unite themselves together. Soon both the maidens opened their eyes and were once more alive. Then they rejoiced, kissed, and hugged each other.

On his return, the wizard at once demanded the keys and the egg, and as he could detect no trace of blood on it, he said, "Thou hast stood the test; thou shalt be my bride."

He now no longer had any power over her and was forced to do whatsoever she desired.

"All right," said she, "but you will first take a basketful of gold to my father and mother and carry it upon your very back. In the meantime, I will prepare for the wedding."

Then she ran to her sisters, whom she had hidden in a little chamber.

"The moment has come when I can save you," said she. "The wretch shall himself carry you home again. But as soon as you arrive you must send help to me."

She put them both in a basket and covered them quite over with gold, until nothing of them was to be seen. Then she called in the wizard to her and said, "Now carry the basket away. But dare not stop for rest along the way, for I shall be watching from my tower window."

The wizard raised the basket onto his back and went on his way. It weighed him down so heavily, though, that the sweat streamed down his face. He then sat down to rest awhile, but immediately one of the sisters cried from the basket, "I am looking through my little window, and I see that you are resting. Go on at once!"

He thought it was his bride who was calling out to him and got up on his feet again. And whenever he stood still, she cried thus, and then he was forced to go onward until, at last, groaning and out of breath, he took the basket with the gold and the two maidens into their parents' house. At his home in the dark woods, however, the bride prepared the wedding feast and sent invitations to all of the wizard's friends. Then she took a skull with grinning teeth, decorated it with gems and a wreath of flowers, carried it upstairs to the garret window, and let it look outward. When all was ready, she climbed into a barrel of honey, and then cut the feather-bed open and rolled herself in it until she looked like a strange bird and no one could recognize her. Then she went out of the house, and on her way, she met some of the wedding guests, who asked:

"Oh, strange bird, from where did you come?"

"Fritz Fitcher's house is where I am from."

"And what may the young bride be doing there?"

"From basement to attic, she's cleaned up the mess, and now from the window she's peeking, I'd guess."

Finally, she met the bridegroom, who was coming slowly back. He, like the others, asked:

"Oh, strange bird, from where did you come?"

"Fritz Fitcher's house is where I am from."

"And what may the young bride be doing there?"

"From basement to attic, she's cleaned up the mess, and now from the window she's peeking, I'd guess."

The bridegroom looked up and saw the decorated skull. He thought it was his bride and nodded to her, greeting her kindly. But when he and his guests had all gone into the house, the brothers and kinsmen of the bride arrived. They had been sent to rescue her, and they locked all the doors of the house that no one might escape. They then set fire to the house, and the wizard and all his crew were burned to death.

The Juniper Tree

Illustrated by Cyrus Rua

Von dem Machandelboom 1812

Originally told to the Grimms by Philipp Otto Runge.

A long, long time ago, most likely some two thousand years or so, there lived a rich man with a beautiful and pious wife. They loved each other dearly but grieved that they had no children. Day and night, the wife prayed, but still they remained childless and barren.

In front of the house there was a yard, in which grew a juniper tree. One winter's day, the wife stood under the tree peeling an apple, and as she peeled it, she cut her finger and the blood fell on the snow.

"Oh," sighed the woman heavily, "if I only had a child, as red as blood and as white as snow." and as she spoke the words, her heart grew light within her, and it seemed that her wish was to be granted.

A month passed, and the snow vanished; after two months, everything had turned to green, and after three, sprouts came from the ground. After four months, the trees budded in the woods, and soon the green branches grew thickly intertwined and the birds began to sing. Their song resounded throughout the forest as the blossoms began to fall. The fifth month found again the wife standing beneath the juniper tree, and it was so full of sweet scent that her heart leaped for joy and she was so overcome with her happiness that she fell

on her knees. When the sixth month had passed, the
fruit became round and firm, and she was at peace,
but when they were fully ripe at the seventh month,
she picked the berries and ate avidly of them, and
then she grew sad and sick. After the eighth month
had passed, she called her husband to
her and wept, "If I die, bury me under
the juniper tree."

Then she felt
content and
relieved,
and before
another month
had passed, she
had a little child
that was as
white as snow
and as red as
blood. And as she
laid eyes upon the
child, her joy was so
great that she died.

Her husband buried
her under the juniper tree
and wept bitterly for her.

Over time, however, his sorrow grew less, and at times he still wept over his loss. After more time passed, he took another wife.

With his second wife, he had a little daughter born to him, while the child of his first wife was a boy, who was as red as blood and as white as snow. The mother loved her daughter very much, and when she looked at the boy, it cut her heart to the quick. She could not forget that he would ever stand be- tween her daughter and her inheritance. Thus, the Devil took  possession of her thoughts more and more and made her behave very unkindly to the boy. She pushed him from place to place, hitting and slapping, so that the poor child went about in constant fear and had no peace from the time he left school to the time he went back.

One day, the little daughter came running to her mother in the storeroom and said, "Mother, give me an apple."

"Yes, my child," said she, and she gave

her a beautiful apple out of a chest that had a very heavy lid and a big, sharp iron lock.

"Mother," said the little daughter again, "may not brother have one too?"

The mother was irritated at this, but she answered, "Yes, as soon as he comes out of school."

And when she looked out of the window and saw him coming up the lane, it seemed as if the Devil entered into her, and she snatched the apple out of her little daughter's hand.

"You shan't have one before your brother," said she and threw the apple into the chest and shut it.

The little boy came through the door, and the evil spirit in the wife made her say kindly to him, "My son, will you have an apple?" yet she gave him a wicked stare.

"Yes please," said the boy, "but my, how ferocious you look!

The thought came to her that she would kill him. "Come with me," said she, and lifted up the lid of the chest. "Take an apple out for yourself."

And as he bent over to do so, the Devil urged her. and *crash!* down went the lid and off went the little boy's head amongst the apples.

Then she was struck with fear and thought, "If only I can keep anyone from knowing that I did it." So she went upstairs to her room and took a white handkerchief out of her top drawer. She set the boy's head again on his neck and bound it with the neckerchief so that nothing could be seen. Whereupon, she placed him on a chair by the door with an apple in his hand.

Soon after this, little Marlinchen, the daughter, came up to her mother who was stirring a pot of boiling water over the fire.

"Mother," said the girl, "brother is sitting by the door with an apple in his hand, and he looks quite pale. I asked him to give me the apple, and he did not respond, and I became very scared."

"Go back to him," said her mother, "and

if he again does not answer, give him a box on the ear."

Little Marlinchen went and said, "Brother, give me that apple," but he did not say a word. So she gave him a box on the ear, and his head rolled off.

She was so terrified at this that she ran crying and screaming to her mother. "Oh!" cried she, "I have knocked off brother's head!" And then she wept and wept and could not be comforted.

"What have you done!" said her mother. "No one must know about this, so you must keep silent. What is done cannot be undone; let us make a stew of him."

She took the little boy and chopped him into pieces, put him in the pot, and let him stew. But Marlinchen stood looking on and wept and wept, until all of her tears fell into the pot, so that there was no need of salt.

When the father came home and sat down at the table, he asked, "Where is my son?"

The mother said nothing but gave him a large bowl of stewed meat, and Marlinchen still wept without ceasing.

The father again asked, "Where is my son?"

"Oh," answered his wife, "he has gone into the country to visit his mother's great uncle; he intends to stay there some time."

"What has he gone there for? He never even said goodbye to me!"

"Well, he wanted to go very badly, and he asked me if he could be away some six weeks. They'll take good care of him."

"I feel very unhappy about it," said the husband. "My permission should have been asked, and he ought to have said goodbye to me."

Then he began his dinner and said, "Little Marlinchen, why do you weep? Brother will soon be back." He then asked his wife for more

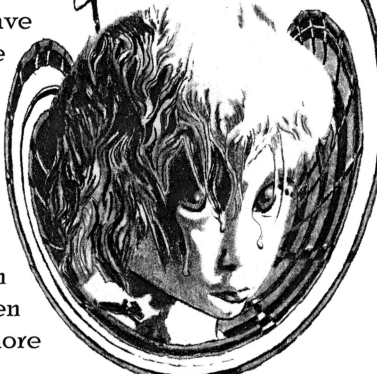

stew, and as he ate, he threw the bones under the table. And the more he ate of it, the more he desired, and was unwilling to share even a bite, somehow feeling that it should be his alone.

Little Marlinchen went upstairs and took her best silk neckerchief out of her dresser, and in it she gathered all the bones from under the table and carried them outside the door. She wept bitter tears as she laid them in the green grass under the juniper tree, and she had no sooner done so, then all her sadness seemed to leave her, and she wept no more.

Now the juniper-tree began to move. The branches separated, and then came together again, as if it might be someone clapping their hands for joy. Whereupon, a mist came round the tree, and in the midst of it, there was a burning as of fire. Out of the fire there flew a beautiful bird that rose high into the air, singing magnificently, and when it vanished, the juniper tree stood there as before, the silk hand-

.

kerchief and the bones gone. Little Marlinchen now felt as happy and gay as if her brother were still alive, and she went back to the house and sat down merrily to the table and ate.

Meanwhile, the bird flew away and alighted on the house of a goldsmith and began to sing:

"My mother killed
      her little son,
Father grieved, but ate
      me when I was gone.
My sister loved me best of all,
Collected the bones
      that soon did fall

Wrapped them in silks, as neat as can be,
Underneath the juniper tree.
Kweet, tweet, what a beautiful bird am I!"

The goldsmith was in his workshop making a gold chain when he heard the song of the bird on his roof. He thought it so beautiful that he got up and ran out, and as he crossed the threshold, he lost one of his slippers. Still, he ran on into the middle of the street, with a slipper on one foot and a sock on the other; he still had on his apron and still held the gold chain and the tongs in his hands. And so he stood gazing up at the bird, while the sun came shining brightly down on the street. "Bird," said he, "how beautifully you sing! Sing me that song again."

"Nay," said the bird, "I do not sing twice for nothing. Give me that gold chain,, and I will sing it for you again."

"All right, here is the chain," said the goldsmith. "Only sing me that song again."

The bird swooped down and took the gold chain in his right claw, and then he landed again in front of the goldsmith and sang:

"My mother killed her little son,
Father grieved, but ate me when I was gone.
My sister loved me best of all,
Collected the bones that soon did fall,
Wrapped them in silks, as neat as can be,
Underneath the juniper tree.
Kweet, tweet, what a beautiful bird am I!"
Then he flew away, and settled on the roof of a shoemaker's house and sang:

"My mother killed her little son,
Father grieved, but ate me when I was gone.
My sister loved me best of all,
Collected the bones that soon did fall,
Wrapped them in silks, as neat as can be,
Underneath the juniper tree.
Kweet, tweet, what a beautiful bird am I!"

The shoemaker heard him, and
he jumped up and ran out in
his shirt-sleeves and stood looking up at the bird on the roof
with his hand over his eyes
to protect them from the sun.

"Bird," said he, "how beautifully you
sing!" Then he called through the door to his
wife, "Darling, come out. Come and hear how
beautifully this bird sings." Then he called
his daughter and her children, then the
apprentices, journeymen, and maid. They
all ran up the street to look at the bird and saw
how splendid it was with its red and green
feathers, its neck glistening like pure gold,
while his eyes sparkled like stars in his head.

"Bird," said the shoemaker, "sing us that
song again."

"Nay," answered the bird, "I do not sing
twice for nothing; you must give me a
present."

"Wife," said the man, "go into the shop
and fetch me the red shoes from the upper
shelf."

And she went in and fetched

the shoes.

"There, bird," said the shoemaker. "Now sing us that song again."

The bird swooped down and took the red shoes in his left claw, flew back to the roof and sang:

"My mother killed her little son,
Father grieved, but ate me when I was gone.
My sister loved me best of all
Collected the bones that soon did fall,
Wrapped them in silks, as neat as can be,
Underneath the juniper tree.
Kweet, tweet, what a beautiful bird am I!"

When he had finished, he flew away. He had the chain in his right claw and the shoes in his left, and he flew far away to a mill. The mill went *clickety-clack, clickety-clack.* Inside the mill were twenty of the miller's men hewing a stone, and as their chisels went *hick-hack hick-hack,* the mill went *clickety-clack, clickety-clack.*

The bird settled on a lime tree in front of the mill and sang:

"My mother killed her little son,"

Then one of the men stopped working.

"Father grieved, but ate me when I was gone."

Then two more stopped to listen.

"My sister loved me best of all,"

Then four more stopped.

"Collected the bones that soon did fall,
Wrapped them in silks, as neat as can be,"

Now but eight remained chiselling.

"Underneath ..."

Now only five.

"... the juniper tree."

Now only one.

"*Kweet, tweet,* what a beautiful bird am I!"

Then he looked up, and the last one had stopped to hear the final words.

"Bird," said the last man, "what a beautiful song that is you sing! Let me hear it too; sing it again."

"Nay," answered the bird. "I do not sing twice for nothing. Give me the millstone, and I will sing it again."

"If it belonged to me alone," said the man, "you could have it."

"If he will sing again," said the others, "he can have it."

The bird came down, and all the twenty millers lifted up the stone with a beam. Then the bird put his head through the hole and took the stone around his neck like a collar and flew back with it to the tree and sang:

"My mother killed her little son,
Father grieved, but ate me when I was gone.
My sister loved me best of all,
Collected the bones that soon did fall,
Wrapped them in silks, as neat as can be,
Underneath the juniper tree.
Kweet, tweet, what a beautiful bird am I!"

And when he had finished his song, he spread his wings, and with the chain in his right claw, the shoes in his left, and the millstone around his neck, he flew straight away to his father's house.

The father, the mother, and little Marlinchen were having their dinner.

"How whimsical I feel," said the father, "so pleased and cheerful."

"Not I," said the mother, "I feel so uneasy, as if a heavy thunderstorm was about to erupt."

And little Marlinchen sat and wept and wept.

Then came the bird flying toward the house and settled on the roof.

"I do feel so happy," said the father. "With the sun shining so beautifully outside, I feel just as if I were going to see an old friend again."

"Not I!" said the wife. "And I am so full of distress that my teeth chatter, and I feel as if there was a fire burning in my veins." She tore open her bodice, and all the while little Marlinchen sat in the corner and wept, and the plate on her knees was wet with her tears.

The bird now flew to the juniper tree and began singing:

"My mother killed her little son,"
The mother shut her eyes and her ears, that she might see and hear nothing, but there was a roaring sound in her ears like a turbulent storm, and her eyes burned and flashed like lightning.

"Father grieved, but ate me when I was gone."
"Look, mother," said the man, "Hearken unto the little bird that so gloriously sings in this sun so warm and air scented of cinnamon!"

"My sister loved me best of all,"
Then little Marlinchen laid her head down on her knees and sobbed, but the man said, "I must go outside and see the bird up close."

"Oh, do not go!" cried the wife. "I feel as if the whole house is shaking and about to go up in flames!"

Nonetheless, the man went out and looked at the bird.

"Collected the bones that soon did fall,
Wrapped them in silks, as neat as can be,
Underneath the juniper tree.
Kweet, tweet, what a beautiful bird am I!"

Upon the dying of the refrain, the bird let fall the gold chain, and it fell round the man's neck so that it fit him perfectly. He went inside, and said, "See, what a splendid bird that is! He has given me this beau-

tiful gold chain, and looks so beautiful himself."

But the wife was in such terror, that she fell to the floor, and her cap fell from her head. Then again the bird began:

"My mother killed her little son,"

"Ah me!" cried the wife. "Would that I were a thousand feet beneath the earth, that I might not hear this!"

"Father grieved, but ate me when I was gone."

Then the woman fell down again as if she was dead.

"My sister loved me best of all,"

"Oh," said little Marlinchen, "I too will go out and see if the bird will give me anything." So out she went.

"Collected the bones that soon did fall,
Wrapped them in silks, as neat as can be,"

And he threw down the shoes to her.

"Underneath the juniper tree.
Kweet, tweet, what a beautiful bird am I!"

And she now felt quite happy and light-hearted. She put on the new red shoes and danced and skipped back into the house, "I was so miserable," said she, "but now I feel so cheerful. That is indeed a splendid bird, and he has given me a pair of red shoes!"

The wife jumped up, and her hair flared as tongues of flame. "Then I will go out too," said she, "and see if it will lighten my misery, for I feel as if the world was coming to an end."

As she crossed the thresh~ old, *crash!* The bird threw the millstone down on her head, and she was crushed to death.

The father and little Mar~ linchen heard the sound and ran back outside, but they only saw smoke and flame and fire rising from the spot. When these had passed, there stood the little brother, and he took the father and little Marlinchen by the hand.

Then they all three re~ joiced, and went inside together and sat down to their dinners and ate.

Terry beal

is the illustrator of *The Maiden Without Hands,*
The Goose Girl, and *Cinderella.* With two decades
of experience in the fine art world, working with
the finest artists and sycophants in the southwest,
Terry's real passion lies in primate discipline. He is
best known, however, for his outer-space airbrush
renderings of alien worlds, and he works as a
master-bassist with such bands as the Soul Poets
and Mr. Noodles.

benedacco

is the illustrator of *Fitcher's Fowl.* He loves
art and music and enjoys being with family,
friends and sundry conscious people.
Seeking to abandon the restaurant business, he is currently enrolled in college,
in spite of his obvious talents as a faith
healer, evidenced by his once making a
blind man lame and even curing a ham.

About the artists

JON FERRILL is the illustrator of *The Poor Boy in the Grave* and *The Singing Bone*. With a degree in computer animation and multimedia from the Dallas Institute of Art, Jon's first love is sculpture, and he's produced everything from 1/64th scale fantasy figurines to visual effects in film. His love of the science-fiction, fantasy, and horror genres shines throughout all of his works regardless of medium, be it ceramic, digital media, paint, pen or ink, and his interests are as diverse as the tools of his trade.

KATHRYN MCLAUGHLIN is the illustrator of *The Twelve Brothers*. A senior at the University of North Texas, her goal is to become a professor of photography at the college level. Her skill in the visual arts has been supported by her family from an early age, and she is enjoying her first successes in gallery exhibition.

LUC HÉBERT is the illustrator of *The Death of the Hen*. A network administrator by day and webmaster and designer by dusk, his folk-art style adds a charming variation to the art presented in the other stories. When not working, Luc enjoys playing guitar, harmonica and singing, as well as watching movies.

karen petroff

is the illustrator of *The Blacksmith and the Devil*. She forsook her acquisition of an art degree from Kent State to start a family, and her current artistic drive is the pursuit of gourmet cuisine. The pieces in this book mark her first return to the fine arts in many years.

Kelly levy

is the illustrator of *The Three Army Surgeons*. She was born the daughter of poor southern sharecroppers from Brooklyn.

Her parents traded her to an insane Belgian named Heinrich when she was seven for a length of rope and a pointed stick. Three days later, she gave Heinrich a broken bottle and half a shoelace for her freedom. Kelly made money killing her fellow drifters for cash as she wandered from town to town. Tired and disoriented, she settled in Virginia thinking it was Canada.

Her hobbies include kicking puppies and buying prescription drugs from unsolicited emails. She owns 28 cats, each one named Mr. Fluffykins.

katy rose

is the illustrator of *The Robber Bridegroom*. Katy has been engulfed in the arts her entire life. Beginning with pencil drawings at a young age, her skills have progressed to encompass paint, pastel, charcoal, and digital media. She is also an accomplished dancer, earning many awards during her 15 years of studio dance experience. Katy is currently pursuing a degree in art and technology at the University of Texas at Dallas and plans to attend graduate school.

the brothers grimm

Jacob Ludwig Carl Grimm (1785-1863) & Wihelm Carl Grimm (1786-1859) were born in Hanau, and both studied law at the University of Marburg. At the beginning of the 19th century, they began collecting the folk tales of the people of Hesse and surrounding regions. In 1812, the brothers Grimm published their first volume of Kinder-und Hausmärchen (Children's and Household Tales) with the second volume following in 1814. 1819 saw them recognized by the University of Marburg with honorary doctorates for their scholarly achievement and they began work on the thirty-two volumes of the Deutsches Wörterbuch German dictionary in 1838, though neither of the brothers lived to see its publication. Tales suppressed & nearly lost under the rule of Napoleon have still found their oppressors long after the Grimm's compilation; German publication of Kinder-und Hausmärchen was banned by Allied commanders after WWII because of their belief that the savagery of the tales helped contribute to Nazi brutality, and the book was in the top hundred most challenged books in United States public schools and libraries in the 1990s.

About the authors

Cyrus Rua is the illustrator of *The Boy Who Went Forth to Learn What Fear Was*, *The Juniper Tree*, *The Mouse, the Bird & the Bratwurst*, and *The Goose Girl*. He is also the sole illustrator of the Lysander Press edition of Oscar Wilde's "The Picture of Dorian Gray." An accomplished artist, actor and musician, Cyrus has produced works for Anne Rice, Mary Black, Drowning Pool's Dave Williams, and Comedy Central. He's appeared on record, screen, and print; been rejected by the Cirque du Soleil, Chuck E. Cheese, and Cameron Diaz, yet was accepted by the Weather Channel.

cyrus rua

CPSIA information can be obtained at www.ICGtesting.com
Printed in the USA
LVOW110018091212

310753LV00011B/429/A